Aberystwyth Boy

A collection of short stories

GWYNN DAVIS

y Lolfa

First impression: 2015

Cover design: Y Lolfa
Cover picture: Gwynn Davis

ISBN: 978 1 78461 120 0

Published and printed in Wales
on paper from well-maintained forests by
Y Lolfa Cyf., Talybont, Ceredigion SY24 5HE
e-mail ylolfa@ylolfa.com
website www.ylolfa.com
tel 01970 832 304
fax 832 782

Contents

The Inventor 7
The Day my Grandfather Died 16
Llangrannog Camp 20
White-Haired Boy 27
Affair of the Heart 34
Uncle Huw's Criminal Past 39
The Amazon Forests 48
Aberystwyth Boy 54
Gareth Makes his Name 68
Uncle Huw 74
The Golfer and his Caddie 81
Saturday Night 94
The Voice of Experience 104

The Inventor

When our family moved to Aberystwyth, my brother Owen was eight and I was nine. Before that we'd lived in Cowes on the Isle of Wight and it was a big change coming to Aberystwyth. School was different for a start, although that was more of a problem for Owen than for me. Owen didn't like school. It had taken him a long time to read and his spelling was terrible. He really couldn't spell at all. His adding up and taking away weren't much good, either. I'm not saying that Owen was stupid – far from it, but it was obvious that he didn't like school work and that moving to a new place upset him.

At the time I wasn't sure why we'd come to Aberystwyth, but looking back on it I think there were two reasons. In the first place my parents thought Owen and I would have a better chance of passing the 11+ exam. I'm not trying to be funny, but I think it was Owen they worried about really. They thought he needed all the help he could get. And I suppose the other reason was that my grandparents lived in Aberystwyth – and then, of course, there was Uncle Huw, who lived a few miles away.

One of the best things about coming to Aberystwyth for Owen and me was the amount of time we were able to spend with Huw. He seemed to have endless patience, and he took a lot of trouble with Owen in particular, helping him with his tables and his spelling. Huw used to stick up for Owen when our father looked at his school books and complained about the untidiness, or the way that all the pages were falling apart.

"Don't keep on at the boy, Meurig," Huw would say. "Owen's

bright enough. One day he'll show you all what a clever lad he is."

"Well I wish he wouldn't keep us waiting," dad would reply.

He was very fond of Owen really; it was just that he didn't have as much patience as Huw. When Owen did finally pass the 11+, you would have thought that dad would be satisfied. But, if anything, things got worse for Owen. It wasn't only dad he had to worry about now; there was old Llew as well. Our new headmaster's name was Mr Llewelyn and everyone called him 'Llew' – behind his back that was. Llew had red hair and a temper to match. He used to drive around Aberystwyth in a very old Ford Anglia, looking out for any of the kids from school walking with their hands in their pockets or slouching along the pavement three abreast so that old ladies had to walk in the gutter. (I only mention that last example because Llew saw me do it once.) He would stop his car and storm over to give you a frightful belt right there in the street. He was a terror.

Owen used to get into trouble with Llew because of the state of his exercise books. Llew said that Owen's was the worst handwriting he'd ever seen.

"Owen Jenkins," he would say, "you're an illiterate half-Welshman and you shouldn't be in my school."

But Owen was a quiet, good-natured boy who never made much fuss and I don't think it bothered him that he was untidy, or if people thought he was stupid. No wonder Huw was fond of him. On the whole I agreed with Huw about Owen. He wasn't stupid at all. In fact, Owen proved towards the end of his first year at grammar school that he was cleverer than the rest of us put together.

It all started one evening when Huw stayed late at our house, helping Owen with his English exercises. I know it was late because Owen and I shared a room and when I went to bed he and Huw were still hard at work. That night Owen had a dream. He told me about it the next morning. He said that in his dream he'd invented a game we could play. Owen tried to explain it to me but it was very complicated and I wasn't sure that I'd understood it properly. He called the game 'Aberystwyth', and to play it you needed the streets in Aberystwyth marked off in squares around the edge of a board: Terrace Road, Pier Street, Great Darkgate Street, and so on. Then each player had some money and you threw dice so that if your counter landed on a street, you could buy it. You could buy and sell streets and the idea was that in the end just one player would own all of Aberystwyth. It sounded to me as if the game had possibilities although, as I say, I'm not sure I understood the finer points.

But when Owen explained the game to my father, he only laughed.

"Not bad, Owen," he said, "but I'm sorry to say someone's got there before you. They call it Monopoly."

"But Owen's game is called 'Aberystwyth'," I said.

"I don't care what he's called it," dad replied, "Monopoly it is, all the same."

But when Huw came to our house that evening and we told him about Owen's new game he was most impressed.

"Owen boy," he said, "this is magnificent. It does bear a passing resemblance to Monopoly, it's true, but all the same, to have invented a game like that is a fine achievement. Don't you think so Meurig?" he said to my father.

"Humph!" dad replied, "some pretty strange dreams going on in this place."

Everyone to whom Owen mentioned the game said how good it was. It was just bad luck that someone had got there before him. Huw said that that happened sometimes with even the most brilliant inventions.

But that wasn't the end of Owen's dreams. Something seemed

to have come over him. About a week later he had another dream. This time he dreamt he was very clever and had wise thoughts. He woke in the middle of this dream and wrote down one of the thoughts he had. He showed it to me the next morning. What Owen had written was: 'Desire can be destroyed' – except he hadn't spelt it quite like that.

I didn't understand what it meant and I don't know that dad did, either.

"What's it mean, Owen?" he said.

"I don't know," Owen replied. "I just dreamt it."

But Huw had the answer. He carefully studied the scribbled note that Owen gave him that evening. Then he closed his eyes and shook his head as if to say that this beat everything.

"What is it, Huw?" I asked.

"The heart of the Buddhist faith, my boy," he replied. "The sum of man's search for wisdom through the ages."

"Has anyone said it before?" I asked Huw.

"Oh yes," he replied, "but no-one knows who; it was thousands of years ago."

"Behind the times again then," dad said.

"But Meurig," Huw said to him, "there isn't a new thought under the sun. It's wonderful that Owen should have dreamt such a thing. You should be proud of the lad."

My father didn't say much but he didn't look proud exactly – puzzled would be more like it.

"Let's see you improve your spelling and punctuation this term, Owen," he said. "I'll swap all your dreams for one decent end-of-term report."

But it looked to me as if Owen was turning into something of a genius. If it had been me I'd have told everyone about my dreams, but he didn't seem to want to do that. And in every other way Owen was as dopey and careless as ever. He still got into trouble because he was so untidy and because he was always forgetting things. One day Llew picked Owen out because he'd forgotten his tie. He told him off in front of the whole class.

But Owen still wouldn't tell anyone about his dreams. I thought it was a shame. I wanted to tell the teachers myself, but Owen wouldn't let me.

"They're only dreams," he said, "and anyway, I haven't dreamt anything new yet."

But Owen's greatest triumph was still to come. A few weeks after he'd dreamt that sentence about Buddhism, he had another dream. It was a scientific dream this time. The morning after it happened, Owen passed me a slip of paper on which he'd written: $E = mc^2$.

"I think it could be important," he said.

"What does it mean?" I asked him. "What's E and what's mc squared?"

"E stands for energy," Owen told me; "m means mass and c is the speed of light."

It didn't mean anything to me, and dad seemed equally nonplussed. As usual only Huw understood the significance of what Owen had written.

"What's he come up with this time?" dad asked when Huw called round to see us that evening.

"The theory of relativity," Huw told him. "You've heard of Einstein, haven't you Meurig?"

"Of course I have," dad replied, "but you can't expect me to recognise the theory of relativity written down. I'd have thought it was longer than that, anyway. Not that I claim to know anything about it, you understand. Neither does Owen, I shouldn't be surprised."

"Of course he understands it," Huw said. "He's written it, hasn't he?"

"It looks too simple," dad said. "Just $E = mc^2$. There must be more to it than that."

"It's not simple at all," Huw replied. "It's a dramatic breakthrough in understanding the laws of physics. Amongst other things, Owen's just re-invented the atom bomb."

"Is that good?" dad asked.

"That's not its only use," Huw told him. "This equation is the basis of our ability to produce great energy from a small mass. Matter into energy… just think of it Meurig, the theory of relativity by an eleven year old. I never thought I'd see the day."

Dad didn't say a lot but he must have been impressed. I kept thinking about the atom bomb. I don't suppose Owen had even heard of it, but now he'd gone and invented it. It made me proud to be his brother.

The dream about relativity was the last that Owen had for a while. The dreams hadn't changed him; he was the same good-natured, absent-minded boy that he'd always been. I couldn't resist telling one or two of my friends about Owen's discovery of relativity, but none of them knew what it was, so they weren't as impressed as I'd hoped. Anyway, even though they didn't know what relativity was, they didn't believe that Owen had discovered it. In the end I told my science teacher.

"Theory of relativity, eh?" he said. "Discovered by Owen, you say. How did he come across it then?"

"He dreamt it," I told him.

"Oh, I might have guessed. A good dreamer is Owen."

Just because Owen was only eleven years old, nobody believed that he could make marvellous discoveries. It shows you how unimaginative most people are.

A long time went by without Owen having any more dreams. I thought he'd stopped completely. I mentioned this to Huw one day.

"Owen's all right," he said to me. "He's a clever lad, but don't ask him to keep proving it. He deserves a rest."

But Owen did have one more dream. It was after a particularly bad thing happened to him in school. One day Llew was addressing the whole school in morning assembly when he spotted Owen talking to another boy from his class. Llew stopped in mid-sentence and there was a terrible silence as he stared down at us from the stage. I didn't know at that moment who it was that had caught Llew's eye and was now the target of his dreadful displeasure. The silence seemed to last for ages, but I suppose it was only a few seconds before Llew spoke:

"Owen Jenkins," he said, "you miserably boy! Go and wait outside my study."

I felt my heart sink to my boots as Owen walked out of the hall to go to Llew's study. He looked a bit thoughtful, but otherwise not much different from usual.

Llew gave Owen six strokes of the cane. I saw Owen afterwards and I could tell he'd been crying, but he didn't say much.

All the same, I'm sure it was as a result of what happened in school that day that Owen had what turned out to be his final inventing dream. He showed me the result next morning. He'd scribbled it on a small piece of rough paper, as he always did. It looked to me like another mathematical formula. There were just five symbols on the paper. They read: beJ^{45}.

"What is it?" I asked him.

"I think it's a new invention," Owen replied, "but I'll need to check with Huw. It's a formula for running motor cars with a new cheap fuel – much cheaper than petrol."

"What's the fuel?" I asked him.

"Horse manure," Owen replied.

I looked at him to see if he was joking, but he didn't seem to be.

"I'm pretty sure it's an original idea," Owen said.

"What do the letters stand for?" I asked him.

"Well, it's a bit technical," Owen said slowly, "but they stand for the different stages by which you convert the manure into the combustible material that drives the engine."

I went to show dad the scrap of paper with the formula on it.

"Look what Owen's done," I said to him, "he's invented a new process for running car engines on horse manure."

Dad looked at Owen. "Doesn't quite compare with the theory of relativity," he said.

"But Owen says it's a new idea," I told him. "We'll need to check with Huw."

"Where are you going to get all that manure?" dad asked.

Owen looked a bit vague for a moment. Then he said: "You wouldn't need much. I think it should be tried on a small scale at first."

Huw called round to see us that evening. He was very excited when he saw the formula.

"It's brilliant, Owen" he said, "just what we need with the price of petrol going up the way it is. What did I tell you, Meurig? I knew Owen would make a breakthrough in the end."

Dad didn't say anything but he didn't look convinced. I wondered how long it would be before the process could be developed and everyone would be running their cars on horse manure. When I asked Huw, he said that it might take quite a long time.

"But anything's possible once the formula's been invented," he said. "All that's necessary now is to build on Owen's idea. I think Mr Llewelyn should be informed – don't you, Owen?"

Owen looked at Huw and I think he smiled.

"Perhaps," he said, "if you think he'd be interested."

When Owen and I walked to school the following morning we happened to see Llew. He was getting out of his old scrapheap of a Ford Anglia in the school car park. I don't know why he didn't get himself a decent car – too mean, I suppose. Then I noticed something that made me stop and look at Owen. But he didn't seem to have noticed.

"What are you staring at Jenkins?" Llew said to me as he passed us.

"Nothing sir," I replied. But when he'd gone I pointed to the registration number of Llew's Ford Anglia.

"Do you see what I see?" I asked Owen.

"Yes," he replied, "BEJ 45 – that's what gave me the idea."

And with that he wandered off to talk to some friends from his class in another part of the playground.

The Day my Grandfather Died

ON THE DAY my grandfather died, my brother Owen and I went to the circus. We had arrived home from school earlier that afternoon to find our mother crying on the stairs. Dad was working fifty miles away, so she was on her own. Even had my father been around, I doubt that mam would have telephoned to ask him to come home: she was independent, something she got from her father, my grandfather, who had died that day. Owen and I stood and looked at her, both of us unhappy and embarrassed, as she struggled to control the tears running down her cheeks. I was ten years old and Owen was nine.

My grandfather had had a bad heart ever since he was a young man, but his death, when it came, was sudden. Everyone was fond of him, but especially my mother, whom he'd loved and protected all her life as if she were still a frail and beautiful child. I was his first grandchild and since I spoke Welsh before I spoke English, I called him 'Tad-cu'. Except that as a baby I couldn't say 'Tad-cu', so I called him 'Tacu' instead. As is the way with childhood mis-pronunciation, he remained 'Tacu' to the end of his life.

I even owe my name to my grandfather. My paternal grandparents had a strong commitment to the Welsh language and Welsh culture – rather too strong a commitment in my mother's opinion. As must often happen in families, especially around the birth of a first grandchild, there was a small disagreement over what I should be called. My grandmother wanted me to be christened 'Taliesin', which is as Welsh as it is possible for any child to be, at least until he is elected archdderwydd.

This proposal distressed my mother, who wrote to the expectant father, still stationed overseas. "Your parents want to call the child 'Machynlleth'," she informed him. This was an exaggeration. Machynlleth is only a few miles up the road from Taliesin, but in terms of their relative acceptability as given names the distance is rather greater than that. Not that a spot of exaggeration ever troubled my mother when her battling instincts were aroused. My paternal grandmother was convinced that her prospective grandchild had poetic leanings. Mam's intuition was different, and closer to the mark: she wasn't confident of my future cultural significance. Accordingly she appealed to her father, my grandfather, who with great reluctance was persuaded to call on dad's parents to discuss the matter. Tacu's fundamental good nature proved impossible to resist and a satisfactory compromise was reached. I was spared Taliesin.

My memories of my grandfather are mainly of the last few years before he died, but my parents have told me other things – for instance, of how he'd say, as I dribbled over him, "Fydd hwn yn ganwr, siŵr" – this one will be a singer for certain – dribbling in babies being taken as a sign of musical talent in Wales. He had a lot of patience with me at a time when I must have needed patience. I never told him I loved him – we didn't tend to say those things in our family – but I suppose it showed in the way I'd seek his company, which is the way kids do show these things. After he'd died I wished I'd told him how I felt, but I suppose he knew.

I used to pester my grandfather to come to church with me on a Sunday evening. The two of us would go together. The service didn't mean much to me, but I used to love the singing and the darkness and the comfort of my grandfather sitting beside me. Later on I would go to watch him play bowls. The strange thing about these memories of my grandfather is that there never seemed to be a time when he didn't want me around. And he was never angry with me, although I know that as a child I did some things that made other grown-ups very angry indeed.

There was the Sunday when my grandfather joined us for lunch. Mam had placed on the table a large bowl of custard as part of our pudding. I was mesmerised by the steaming yellow liquid and, before anyone could stop me, I picked up the bowl and poured the custard over my head. The custard was scalding hot, and I screamed – partly from pain and partly from fear of the retribution to come. Mam was crying as hard as me, and it fell to my grandfather to clean up the mess, which was considerable, and also to protect me from the punishment that was my due. His manner of dealing with such catastrophes may be discerned from his cheery greeting when I saw him next: "Shw ma'r dyn bach melyn?" – 'How's the little yellow man'?

I still have a picture of my grandfather in my mind. It's taken from the way he looked in a photograph in the bowling club. He had an oval face with thin, white hair and a rather grim expression around his mouth, perhaps from being in pain. But there seemed to be great kindness in his face. That is something I've often thought about when I myself have done mean or stupid things. I probably disappointed him at times, and I would imagine him looking at me with those tired eyes. However badly I behaved, it was always a comfort to think of my grandfather's eyes upon me.

When mam broke the news to Owen and me, I think she wanted some comfort from us – a sign that we shared her distress. But I was only conscious of her misery and of how it made me feel uncomfortable. My loss seemed unimportant beside hers – as perhaps it was. I didn't say anything. I didn't cry. I just felt depressed and awkward, as I think did Owen, shuffling beside me.

We had tickets for the circus that evening. It was the same circus that came to Aberystwyth every year, but this was the first time Owen and I had been allowed to go. Mam hated circuses because she thought they were cruel to animals, but she must have given in to our badgering.

I asked her if we were still going to go to the circus.

"Do you still want to?" she said to me.

I looked at Owen, who said nothing.

"Yes," I said.

I know it didn't help my mother at the time, and in later years I regretted not staying at home with her that evening. But I was only ten, and there was more unhappiness on that stairwell than I could cope with. The greater loss was my mother's, of that I have no doubt, but for Owen and me, no-one had told us that our grandfather wouldn't always be around. Now we knew, and the sadness of that fact lay all about us, permitting no escape. Yes, we went to the circus, and since it was my first and last time you'd think I would have some memory of it. But there's nothing. All I remember of that evening is my mother crying on the stairs.

Llangrannog Camp

ABERYSTWYTH AIRPORT MUST have the shortest runway in the world. It calls for considerable pilot resolution, coupled with an impressive local knowledge, to even contemplate bringing a plane to rest on that absurdly truncated and precipitous landing strip. So difficult is it, in fact, that one might almost say that Aberystwyth airport doesn't have a runway. Or to put it another way, Aberystwyth, as many of you are probably aware, doesn't really have an airport. But once you start to build a dream world in which you are recognised as someone out of the ordinary, you never want to leave it. And when I was a small boy, recently arrived in Aberystwyth, I wanted to be an airline pilot. I'd imagine my plane stricken with engine failure and me bringing it safely down in a crash-landing of unprecedented skill and courage. Later, when it became apparent that I wasn't going to *be* an airline pilot, I'd imagine I was a passenger in a plane when some dreadful emergency would mean I was called to the controls: such as the crew having simultaneous heart attacks, or being shot by a hijacker who then committed suicide. I didn't have much concern for the crew in these fantasies of mine.

The later versions involved my being in communication with the control tower, as I'd need to be taught how to fly the plane. I'd be 'talked down', coolly following the instructions I was given by the flight controller. I suppose nowadays they'd come with all sorts of reasons for my wanting to be in charge of a jet aircraft. I think I just wanted the attention.

Then there were my rugby-playing exploits. I first played rugby when I was eleven, which was an especially active time for my fantasies. I spent more time daydreaming than I did in the real world. As it happened I was quite a good player: easily scared, but fast. I weighed little over five stones, which made me a little vulnerable to the rough stuff, but they used to put me on the wing where I wasn't likely to get hurt. I managed to scamper through for some tries in our weekly games lesson at school and I even played for our first-year team, called the Bantams.

But I dreamed of greater things. Even then I followed the fortunes of the Welsh rugby XV and of the British Lions on tour in New Zealand at the time. I used to dream of being called upon to play for the Lions in their hour of need…

It was the time of the final Lions Test match which would decide the series. The Lions had been badly hit by injury. Rather unwisely the management had flown all the injured players' home, leaving only the fifteen who were to play in the Test. I happened to be on holiday with my parents in Auckland at the time – the details in that respect were a little hazy; anyway, the point is that I was there.

On the morning of the match, one of the Lions team – a winger as it happened – fell down the stairs of the team hotel and broke his leg. A desperate team manager put out a call on New Zealand radio, appealing for any British rugby player in the vicinity to report to the team's hotel. I went along, naturally, and was shown in to the see the manager.

"What position do you play, son?" he asked me.

"On the wing, sir."

"Hm. You're a bit small. How old are you, anyway?"

"Eleven, sir."

"Who do you play for?"

"Ardwyn Grammar School Bantams."

"Well, we don't seem to have anyone else. I'll put you in on the wing – but you're to keep out of trouble. Just use your speed when you get the chance."

"Yes, sir."

The rest is history. The Lions, with magnificent covering, managed to make up for my defensive deficiencies on the left wing. New Zealand had scored just one penalty, but it seemed that it would be enough. With five minutes of the match remaining, they led by three points to nil. Now they were attacking our line again. They passed the ball along the three-quarters and suddenly I was faced with two men bearing down on me. Just as I did in games lessons at school, I shirked the tackle and went for the interception. They fell for it. I caught the ball and was away. Racing over the halfway line, I had the whole New Zealand team behind me, but I was too fast to be caught. I ran the length of the pitch and flung myself over the try line. I'd scored the winning try in the final Test. It was the only time I'd touched the ball in the whole game.

How many of us have the capacity, given the absolute right circumstances, for one brief moment of genius which would transform our lives? All of us, I guess. Aged eleven or twelve, I was hungrily waiting for my moment to arrive. It seemed to take a long time. But one stupendous summer's day, when I was still only twelve years old, it finally came – I moved from the world of my imagination into a triumph in real life. I'll tell you how it happened.

It was 1960, the year that throwing the frisbee became a craze in America. The frisbee soon became popular in Britain too, and in the summer of that year it was possible to see kids of all ages throwing the frisbee to one another on beaches and across other open spaces. A good frisbee has aerodynamic qualities so that if thrown well – that is, smoothly, flat to the ground and with plenty of spin – it can be thrown long distances and with great accuracy.

A lot of the boys in Aberystwyth were learning how to throw the frisbee that summer, but none of them practised as hard as

I did. Owen and I threw the frisbee to one another in our back garden. We would stay there for hours. It was a great delight to send the frisbee curving away from Owen and for him to stand there totally confident that the spin which I had imparted would bring it swooping into his stomach. Unfortunately Owen was a bit clumsy, so he didn't always catch it.

At other times I would practise throwing the frisbee for distance. My parents had bought me a heavy American frisbee which was difficult to throw but once you got the turn of the wrist just right and released it with the right amount of spin, only a foot or so above the ground, it would fly for fifty yards or more.

It was in August of that year that I went to stay for one week at a children's summer camp at Llangrannog, which is a small village on the Cardiganshire coast. It was a big camp with over a hundred boys aged from twelve to fifteen. I was one of the youngest there, and the homesickness was overpowering. What saved me was that every day the teachers organised a sporting event of one kind or another. On the second morning of the camp it was announced that on the final day, just before our departure, there would be a frisbee-throwing competition, to be held on the main rugby pitch. Best of all, we were told that Terry Davies, the Welsh full-back at the time who played for Llanelli, would be visiting the camp that morning in order to supervise the competition.

The sun shone that week, and each evening, after the day's main activities were over, some of the boys would take their frisbees outside in the evening sunshine and practise throwing to one another. Some of the bigger boys could throw a long way, but I thought I might have a chance against them because I understood throwing the frisbee better than they did. They were stronger than me, but strength isn't everything when throwing the frisbee, although a lot of people think it is. It's more important to get a fast flick of the wrist and a smooth, flat release so that the frisbee carries on the wind. It was very windy on the cliff top at Llangrannog.

On the final morning of the camp the teachers explained the rules of the frisbee competition and then we all raced out on to the rugby pitch. We were each to have one throw. Terry Davies was introduced to us and I can remember thinking what big hands he had and how he could probably throw the frisbee out of sight. I half expected him to make a speech, which is what I'd have done if I were him, but he seemed rather quiet considering what an important person he was. He went and stood by the try line from which we would each have to take our throw, ready to start the competition. I can remember that it was sunny, but there was a strong wind blowing. I was listed as one of the last to throw.

I watched eagerly as the competition got under way and the boys near the top of the list took it in turns to throw. Most of them fell short of the 25-yard line, their frisbee blown by the wind and curving away on its side to dip sharply to the ground. But there were some good throwers amongst the older boys and one boy, Huw Morgan, who was the best table-tennis player at the camp, sent a lovely flat long throw dipping across the wind to land nearly fifty yards away.

I pulled back my arm in a couple of practice swings. The wind had changed direction slightly so that it was coming at an angle from behind the throwers. I knew that it was a very good wind for throwing a frisbee, if only the spin and the angle of release were right. I watched the others throw. Some of the boys threw too high and the wind came up under the frisbee, turning it on its side so that it fell to the ground only a few yards from where they stood. It was an easy mistake to make.

Then it was my turn. I stood at my mark, hoping for an especially strong gust of wind. As I stood there I went over in my mind what I had to do: a curving run up, then the frisbee drawn back and released with hard wrist spin, left-hand lip slightly nearer to the ground to take advantage of the wind. I heard Terry Davies shout "Go!" and as he did so I sensed the breeze freshening behind me. I started my run-up and almost threw myself across the line as I released a low hard throw. Then I watched my frisbee as it flew dead level over the ground, not rising or falling, but skimming on the wind.

It sailed past the judges with the measuring tape on the halfway line, still riding flat and true on the wind. Then it began to slow as the power I had given left it, but still flat to the ground it drifted on, eventually coming to rest at the foot of the far goalposts, a hundred yards away. For a moment there was silence and then I became aware, as if from a long way away, of the whistles and shouts of the other boys. I looked up and saw some of them rushing towards me. I was pushed and shoved and slapped on the back. I heard Terry Davies say: "Look out, he's only a little 'un", and then I felt myself lifted from the crowd. I saw Huw Morgan, who grinned at me and stuck his fist in the air...

Of course, knowing what a dreamer I am, some of you may suspect that this was just another of my fantasies, only with a bit more detail this time. To tell you the truth, I've had the same thought myself. After all, there was no trophy or newspaper report to prove what I'd done. After the passage of so many years, I began to suspect that perhaps I'd imagined the whole thing.

Then, last summer, I decided to set my mind to rest. I went back to Llangrannog. I could vaguely remember the hilltop, overlooking the sea, but I had to enquire of a local shopkeeper before I managed to find the path that led to the camp. The climb was a struggle, but at last I clambered over the gate at the top and there, laid out before me, were row upon row of huts, creosote brown, the same huts in which we'd slept some fifty years before. Beyond them was the field, rather smaller than I remembered it, but still with that slope towards the sea over which my frisbee had slipped with such easy grace, like a gull that had forgotten to land.

I was in no hurry. I walked the perimeter of the field and then stopped to look out over the bay. As I stood there I felt the breeze freshening against my cheek, and it seemed to me that it was exactly the same breeze. Then, although I was alone on the field, I heard the shouts of a hundred boys. And I knew that I could not possibly have been mistaken.

White-Haired Boy

ROBIN PRITCHARD WAS a white-haired boy, and that one identifying feature – Robin's shock of white hair – is what stays with me. For I didn't know him well. Robin was two years younger than me, which is a lot when you are both at primary school, and by the time I got to Ardwyn, Robin was no longer around. But my brother Owen knew Robin. Robin was the first boy to speak to Owen when we arrived at our new primary school, and they became friends. I'm not sure what drew them together. When aged eight or nine, Owen spent much of his time in grave contemplation – no-one knew for certain of whom or of what. Robin also stood out from the general run of boys, but whereas Owen was thoughtful and reserved, Robin was sparky and elusive. He couldn't have weighed more than four stone, and he was never still.

Robin and Owen would climb trees together in Cwm Woods, about a mile from our house. The only time I can remember Robin addressing me directly was in those woods. I was on my way home, and the woods were a short-cut. Suddenly I heard a child's voice, "Hello Gareth!" The salutation was cheery, and perhaps slightly mocking. For there was no-one to be seen. I looked about me, but could see only trees. Then the voice called again – "Hello!" – and because I was better prepared this time I spotted the direction from which the sound came. I wandered off the path to my right, and looked up. High above me, amongst the fragile upper branches of possibly the tallest tree in the whole wood, I glimpsed a shock of white hair. I called back – "Hello Robin!" – but there was no response other than a rustle of branches. I continued on my way. It was plain that Robin was not in any difficulty – his greeting had been an expression of sheer exuberance.

Owen didn't attempt Robin's more hair-raising escapades, but since Robin could not walk home from school without clambering over various obstacles, Owen was bound to be drawn in. One of Robin's tricks was to edge his way along a narrow pipe that crossed a brackish stream that wound its way through the park that separated the football ground from the council houses on the edge of town. The pipe was six inches across, and it was suspended about ten feet above the water, which was only a few inches deep. On one occasion Owen had attempted to follow his friend, and he'd fallen in. He arrived home from school muddy and stinking, with a badly-sprained ankle. Mam was furious. She hauled Owen's clothes off and threw them straight in the washing machine as he stood shivering and miserable in the kitchen. "Get in the bath, Owen," she said, "and begin scrubbing. I'll be along to inspect you shortly."

Owen learned from that experience. I think he realised that Robin's affinity with heights was one that he himself could not hope to match. So whenever Robin attempted one of his gravity-defying escapades, Owen would watch his friend from ground level. One of Robin's favourite haunts was Constitution Hill, the crumbling lump of rock that overlooks the sea on the north side of town. Owen and I both enjoyed exploring the cliff walk from Aberystwyth north to Clarach, and then, if the sun shone and time permitted, further north to Borth. But Robin was not content to stay on the path, or for that matter to explore the woodland and fields further inland. He preferred to clamber down the cliff face, where the gulls and other sea birds would wheel about his head. One of Robin's tricks was to disappear over the edge of the cliff, goat-like, as if stepping off the edge of the world. The crumbling shale of Constitution Hill could not be relied upon, but such was Robin's affinity with the rock, Owen told me later that he'd never known him dislodge a single pebble.

Mam and dad were pleased that Owen had found a new friend, and they liked Robin. They had even invited him to join us on a family holiday that we were planning to take in New Quay later that summer. New Quay is just down the Cardiganshire coast from Aberystwyth, but for Owen and me it had a deep and abiding attraction. We'd spent a few days there every summer when we'd returned to Wales, and we enjoyed it so much that we never wanted to go anywhere else. Robin lived with his grandparents, and he'd confessed to Owen that he'd never had a holiday, so this summer, for the first time, Robin was going to accompany us.

But although my parents were fond of Robin, they knew he was a daredevil, and they feared that where he led, Owen could well follow. I think it was mam who persuaded our dad to have a word with Owen. This he did one sunny evening in early June, when he spotted Owen leaving the house without telling any of us where he was going. Dad followed Owen outside.

"Where are you going, Owen?" dad asked him.

"Consti."

'Consti' was Constitution Hill.

"On your own?" dad enquired. Owen guessed what was coming, but he knew better than to attempt to lie to our dad.

"No – with Robin."

"Where's Robin now?"

"Outside, waiting for me."

"Ask him to come in for a minute."

Reluctantly Owen went to fetch his friend. A minute or so later Robin appeared at our front door. He was hopping from one foot to another, and I could see he was nervous.

"Hello Robin," dad said, "how are you today?"

"Very well thank you Mr Jenkins."

"Going climbing?"

Robin glanced at Owen, who adjusted his features to their most carefully non-committal. Robin did his best given the lack of guidance offered.

"Maybe," he said, "depending what's there."

"Well the cliff is probably still there, Robin," dad said, "but I want you to listen to what I'm going to say to Owen."

Dad turned to Owen, and I could see that he was thinking carefully what to say.

"Owen," he began, "I want you to have a good time, but I'd prefer it, on balance, if you didn't break every last bone in your body."

Owen looked at dad enquiringly – this was an unusual speech.

"Those cliffs are dangerous – the rock is too poor for climbing. I'd say the same to Robin, except it's not my place to do that. But I am saying it to you. I'm happy for you to go with Robin, but I don't want you on those cliffs. Is that understood?"

Owen nodded, and I could see that dad, having made what for him was an uncharacteristically sombre speech, wanted to lighten the mood.

"And don't think you can disobey me just because you're out of my sight. I have my spies. And if they ever report seeing you near those cliffs, I will personally throw you over the edge. So don't make me do it – it would upset your mother."

Owen's eyes lit up as he glimpsed an opportunity for mischief. The paradoxical nature of the threatened punishment was all too evident, and Owen was inclined to debate the point. But one glance at dad was sufficient for him to think better of it. He nodded once more before turning to accompany Robin down the path to our front gate. I followed dad indoors. Out of the corner of my eye I saw Robin give a little skip as he bounded down the road.

There were only a further two weeks of school before the summer holidays, and Owen and I were both looking forward to the weeks of idleness that stretched unendingly ahead. On the first Saturday after school broke up, our parents took us to visit friends of theirs who lived in the Carmarthenshire village of Dre-fach. Owen was restless: it wasn't how he'd planned to start the holiday.

"You'll enjoy it when you get there," dad said.

"I'll enjoy it here," Owen had replied. But dad had insisted.

"Tell Robin you'll meet him tomorrow," he said.

The sun shone that day, but the atmosphere was humid and there were distant rumbles of thunder as we played in our friends' garden. As we began the journey home the skies darkened, and dad was soon driving with his headlights on. We'd got as far as Lampeter when the storm broke. We drove the rest of the way home in lashing rain, Owen and I transfixed by the flashes of lightning and the booming thunder that followed almost immediately as the storm raged overhead. By the time we reached Aberystwyth the rain had eased, but as dad drove up the final steep hill to our house, streams of water were running down both sides of the road. Dad had to steer between the potholes that had been newly-created by the force of the rain as it removed loose stones from the pitted surface. It had been quite a storm.

An hour or so later, as mam prepared our tea, Owen and I heard a thump-thump sound overhead, so we wandered out on to the wooden veranda that bordered our house on its western side. From there we had a good view of the town below, and of the sea. The noise was that of a helicopter that flew over the northern edge of town before settling to hover over Constitution Hill. The helicopter, which was bright yellow in colour, stayed in the one spot for several minutes. Then it flew north, out of sight of our house in the direction of Clarach, before returning once more to hover over the cliffs in clear view of our house. It was an unusual sight, and walkers going past our house on the way to the golf course stopped to stare. The helicopter remained in the same spot for fifteen to twenty minutes before finally heading south across the bay. Owen and I watched until it became a tiny speck against the south Cardiganshire coast, then disappeared altogether.

*

New Quay that summer felt different from previous summers, but perhaps that's because Owen and I were different. Owen didn't say much at the best of times, but he was even quieter than usual. The weather was disappointing, but we still went to the beach most days. Mam fussed a lot – she didn't want us to swim beyond the harbour wall, and when we did go for a swim she always followed. I don't know what she imagined she was going to do – rescue us if we got into difficulties, I suppose, but since mam was a terrible swimmer it wasn't clear how she was going to manage that. She swam breaststroke, but insisted on keeping her hair dry, which pushed her body upright in the water so there was no forward propulsion. Owen and I found ourselves swimming around her, like tugs circling a stately ocean liner, as mam made her gentle forward pushing motions, all the time seeking to ensure that she kept the two of us in view. "Do you do life-saving?" Owen whispered to me at one point, "because I think you may have to".

Dad did what he did every day at home when he wasn't at work – he read the newspaper, and then settled down to re-read his favourite novels – Simenon, Marquand, or Raymond Chandler. He also tried to teach Owen and me to play chess.

Owen had little interest in the game, and was forever exposing his Queen to capture, but dad and I played a game of chess most days. We also played a nightly game of cards – Rummy or Strip Jack Naked. This was a family ritual, but only dad and I were really interested. Mam couldn't concentrate, so she never remembered what cards had gone, and it was plain that Owen didn't care whether he won or lost.

We also went on trips, mainly to other coastal resorts, but also inland to places dad remembered from his childhood, ones that he was eager to tell us about. The only one I can remember was a visit to a distant cousin of dad's, who lived near Newcastle Emlyn. She was a very old lady, who was rumoured within the family to be rich. "Got to safeguard the inheritance," dad said. That proved to be our last day. When we woke the following morning it was raining hard, so we decided to come home.

*

All this was a very long time ago, and of course I viewed the events of that summer through a child's eyes. I suppose we were resilient, although perhaps I shouldn't speak for Owen. Boys of that age keep a great many things to themselves. I've sometimes wondered how he managed, and whether he was more upset than I realised.

As for me, I still struggle to make sense of things. It isn't that I've been plagued by ill-fortune in my own life – not at all. There have been some buffetings, but for the most part I've got over them, and I see others who have had to cope with incomparably worse. There are even times as I get older when I feel I'm getting the hang of things. But that feeling doesn't last. It's been over fifty years since Robin's accident, but mostly I feel the same now as I did when I was eleven. Which is to say, that life doesn't make any sense at all.

Affair of the Heart

WE'D BEEN LIVING in Aberystwyth for less than a year when my mother attended her first evening class. It was an art class, and the teacher was the same long-suffering man who taught art at the grammar school. He confided to me some years later that my mother's pictures resembled an explosion at a confetti factory. I don't think he communicated this to her directly. Mam seemed quite proud of her foray into the art world.

There followed a whole series of evening classes – ancient civilisations, French (her only admitted failure) and finally, history of science. Mam took to science, and above all, she took to biology. She became, you might say, biologically obsessed. That at least was my Uncle Huw's opinion. I sometimes thought that mam only went to evening classes so that, just for once, she would know more about some subject than Huw. Sadly for her, it transpired that Huw knew quite a bit of biology.

Huw happened to be round at our house on the night of my mother's final history of science evening class. When mam came home, at about nine o'clock, our dad, my brother Owen, Huw and I were all sat in the living room, watching television.

"What was it tonight, mam?" I asked her.

"Blood," mam replied. "Did you know, Gareth, that it was in the 17th century that man first realised that blood circulated round the body?"

"William Harvey, 1628."

That was Huw's voice, spoken from behind his newspaper, where he'd retreated when my mother entered the room. Mam ignored him, but I could see that she wasn't pleased at his intervention. It wasn't very tactful of Huw.

"I bet Doctor Williams doesn't know that," dad said.

Doctor Williams was our GP. He'd been to school with dad, who didn't have a high opinion of his abilities.

"I bet he hasn't heard of the circulation of the blood."

"Don't be ridiculous, Meurig," mam said.

In an effort to smooth things over, I asked my mother: "What did they think happened before they knew it was the circulation?"

Rather to my surprise, mam looked disconcerted at that. There were chuckles from behind the newspaper. Then she seemed to recover herself: "Don't you worry about that, Gareth. The important thing is we know now. We know the blood circulates because in the blood is a substance called haemoglobin. Haemoglobin carries oxygen. Our bodies need oxygen. Every single cell needs oxygen. Only by the blood circulating oxygen around the body can our cells survive."

It was then that Huw piped up again. I couldn't always tell when he was being serious, but he'd put down his newspaper and he had the air of a man genuinely seeking knowledge.

"What makes the heart pump?" he asked mam.

She said: "I've just explained that – I thought you knew it all anyway."

"No, I'm not asking what purpose it serves," Huw replied. "What I want to know is – what prompts the heart to do this pumping business? Don't tell me that the heart actually *decides* that the cells in the body need oxygen – although I don't dispute for a moment that they do need the stuff. What motivates the heart, if I may put it another way, into doing all this pumping? I know we'd be in a mess if it stopped, but what makes the heart pump?"

Mam's face had become a little red and blotchy at this last

speech of Huw's. She looked to my father, as if for support, but all dad said was: "Rhodri Pugh would like an answer to that." Rhodri Pugh was a member of dad's bowling club who'd dropped dead from a heart attack a few weeks previously.

Mam turned back to Huw: "All right then Mister Know-it-all, you tell me what makes the heart pump."

Huw seemed to have been expecting that.

"Yes, well, I've been thinking about it – just for the last couple of minutes, you understand. The heart pumps because it is squeezed by the lungs."

Mam looked at Huw very hard for a second, and then she made as if to leave the room, observing dismissively to the four of us: "That's the daftest thing I've ever heard in my life."

"No, listen Megan," Huw said, looking sideways at me. "What do you call the inside of your chest, the hole which has the lungs in it?"

"The thoracic cavity," mam said. I could tell she was pleased that she'd remembered it.

"Right!" said Huw, as if this helped to prove his argument. "And what other major organ is to be found nestling in the thoracic cavity?"

"The heart, of course."

"Right! The heart and lungs are both to be found in the thoracic cavity, nestling snugly side by side. Now then, what happens when you breathe in? Your lungs expand," Huw said, not waiting for a reply to his own question. "As you breathe, your lungs expand and contract; they expand when you breathe in and they contract when you breathe out. Now then, Megan, when you breathe in…" Here Huw held an exaggerated dramatic pause… "When you breathe in, the lungs expand, pushing against the heart. The heart is then *squeezed* (heavy emphasis from Huw) … the heart is *squeezed* between the lungs and the wall of the thoracic cavity. This alternate squeezing and then releasing of the heart by the lungs is what produces the pumping action of the heart which then propels the blood with your precious haemoglobin in it around the body. This is a purely mechanical action, identical in principle to the way in which, when I have a puncture on my bicycle, I manipulate the bicycle pump."

I thought mam was going to burst.

"Stop it!" she cried. "You haven't got a clue about the operation of the human body. You've dreamed up this rubbish just to upset me."

Huw looked at her rather slyly, and he winked at me.

"Then tell me, Megan," he said, "why does the jolly old heart pump?"

"All right," mam conceded. "I don't know. But neither do you, you old fraud. I'll check with my science teacher."

"You do that girl, assuming you can get hold of him. But I observe that the course finished tonight without this somewhat vital bit of information being offered. It suggests to me..." Huw paused and looked at mam triumphantly "... that the blighter jolly well doesn't know. Just decided to pass the matter off, hoped no-one would notice. It worked, too. But not with me. Too smart for him."

"I refuse to discuss the subject any further," mam said.

"Fair enough," Huw replied, "but I've got proof if you want to hear it. On the other hand perhaps we'd better leave it, as you suggest."

"What proof?" mam asked, unable to resist.

"Well," said Huw, "did you by any chance happen to see Rhodri Pugh, after he'd snuffed it the other week?"

"You know I didn't," mam replied, in such a way as to suggest that she'd lost patience with his silly games.

"Well, it so happens," said Huw, "that I did. And what's more, there were one or two things, being an observant chap, that I happened to notice. First… (another significant pause from Huw)… he wasn't breathing. I want you to make a note of that important fact, Megan – *not* (emphasis) breathing. Second (another pause, as Huw looked at mam from beneath raised eyebrows)… his heart, bless him, had stopped."

"Yes," mam said, "of course it had."

"Well, that's it," Huw said, "there's your proof."

"What do you mean, 'that's it'?"

"Just what I say: breathing stopped; lungs stopped pressing against the heart; heart stopped pumping; Rhodri Pugh no longer with us. I'm sorry girl. I've seen the evidence."

"Huw," mam said to him, "if you don't admit right now that what you've been saying this past ten minutes is complete and utter rubbish, you'll leave the house this instant. I've had enough of your nonsense."

"Bit of a problem for a chap, that," said Huw, getting slowly to his feet, "when he's seen the evidence."

Huw winked at Owen and me as he made his way to the front door.

"See you later, boys," he said, and then, with a meaningful look in mam's direction: "Don't forget now, Megan – keep breathing."

With that, Huw let himself out, and Owen and I were packed off to bed, a little more abruptly than usual.

The following day mam had a card from Huw, and a little note which I didn't read. But I think he must have said he was sorry because he was round at our house again the following week.

Uncle Huw's Criminal Past

UNCLE HUW, MY father's older brother, must have been about forty-five years old when we moved back to Aberystwyth, but to me he seemed older. His face was heavily lined and he had a deep base voice which was something of a surprise at first, coming as it did from such a thin, wiry man, not much over five foot six inches tall. I was frightened of Huw to begin with; he would look so stern and he talked so quick – I jumped whenever he asked me a question. But I came to recognise that he was a kindly man, if a little short-tempered at times.

Huw's background was something of a mystery to me. He didn't seem to work, and he lived on his own in a cottage on the edge of Bow Street, a village just north of Aberystwyth. I used to cycle out to see him, and he would always greet me warmly and offer me chocolate biscuits. I couldn't help noticing that Huw's cottage was rather grubby, at least in comparison with our house, which mam ensured was spotless. Also, in hot weather Huw's living room could be a bit smelly, whilst in winter, when it was cold outside, the cottage was freezing. There seemed to be radiators, but they were never switched on. In the winter Huw would wear an overcoat and gloves indoors. It wasn't easy for visitors, but I don't believe Huw had many of those.

I once asked Huw why he never switched the central heating on. He said it was because he didn't feel the cold, but since he was wearing an overcoat indoors at the time I don't think that can have been right. I could have asked my mother, but I knew she and Huw didn't get on. I think the problem was that Huw liked to tease my mother, and mam didn't like being teased. She said to me once: "Whatever that man tells you, don't believe a word of it." It would have felt disloyal to Huw to ask her about him.

It was after I'd cycled out to Bow Street a good many times that Huw took me into his confidence.

"You know, Gareth," he said to me one day, "not everything is as it seems. Sometimes things happen you can't control, and then you just have to make the best of it. That's what I'm trying to do – make the best of it."

"Make the best of what, Huw?" I asked him.

"Of my life," Huw replied. He looked at me carefully, as if trying to decide whether it was wise to continue. He must have decided it was safe to do so, because after a brief pause he went on…

"You see Gareth, a few years ago I had a problem. Has Meurig told you about it?"

I shook my head.

"No, I don't suppose he would. Well, if you're interested, I'll tell you. I haven't always been unemployed, you know. I had a good job once. I was in charge of security at a large London department store. It was a responsible position, and I enjoyed it. If ever there was a problem in the store, I was the person they came to. Then one winter – it was over fifteen years ago, so before you were born – I began to have a problem. It was the strangest thing, Gareth; for some reason I became unable to stand the central heating at work. I'd get into the office in the morning and although the temperature was the same as normal, I felt as though I couldn't breathe – that I was on the verge of suffocating."

Huw paused and looked at me reflectively before continuing.

"There was no need to tell me that it was all my imagination; I knew that myself, but it didn't stop the way I felt. I got so desperate that I turned off the central heating in my room – though this was in November and it was beginning to get really cold. My office was like an ice box, but it was the only way I could bear to be in the place. Everyone who came to see me complained about the cold, but I just couldn't turn the heating back on. It's a strange thing, Gareth, isn't it? I don't suppose you've ever heard of anyone having such a problem before?"

I shook my head. For a while Huw seemed lost in thought. When eventually he continued, he spoke slowly, as if it pained him to recall certain events.

"But then I had an idea. My office had a hearth and what had obviously at one time been a coal fire. I made discreet enquiries and discovered that the chimney was still open. That's when I made my big mistake."

Huw paused again.

"Go on, Huw," I said.

"Well, I decided to light a coal fire in my room. It was against regulations, but since I was the regulations around that place I didn't think anyone would complain. It wasn't as though there would be any real danger. The fireplace hadn't been used for years, but the chimney was in good working order. I bought a bag of coal and stocked up with wood chippings and then, when I would arrive in the mornings, I'd get a nice blaze going.

I was careful, of course. I got a fire guard and I made sure the fire was properly out when I left in the evening. No-one complained. In fact most people liked the cosy atmosphere in my room. I even got a nice piece of carpet to put down. I didn't tell anyone about my dislike of central heating. I couldn't understand it myself, and there are some things you don't like to talk about.

For a time all was well, but then, Gareth, I began to experience another problem. This second thing that happened to me was much more serious. You might even say it changed my life. I was dialling a number at work – I remember to this day that it was a building firm I needed to contact in order to get them to do a few repairs on the ground floor. And you know, Gareth…" Huw took a deep breath, and when he resumed speaking it was very, very softly, so much so that I had to lean forward to catch what he was saying.

"I couldn't dial the number. I don't mean that the telephone wasn't working, or that the number was engaged. I mean that I couldn't put my finger on certain numbers on the telephone dial. It was the high numbers I couldn't manage. In those days we didn't have push button telephones – you had to turn the telephone dial by putting your finger in the hole that corresponded to the number you wanted. I was trying to dial 32280 as I recall. I dialled 322 without any difficulty, but for some reason my eyes wouldn't take in the high numbers. You know how the numbers used to go on a telephone? Clockwise from the bottom they'd go 0987 and so on round to 1, which was on the right hand side. I had no trouble looking at the numbers on the right – the low numbers – but I couldn't bring my eyes to shift across, so it was impossible for me to put my finger in any of the holes on the left-hand side of the dial. It seemed a huge distance across the telephone dial from right to left; I couldn't bridge it."

My eyes must have been standing out of my head, because Huw looked concerned. "Don't worry, Gareth," he said, "I'm over it now, but at the time it had some unfortunate consequences."

"What consequences, Huw?"

"Well, not wanting to turn on the central heating could be regarded as a minor eccentricity, but this new problem made it almost impossible for me to do my job. What were people supposed to think? It's one thing not to like central heating, but you never hear of someone not being able to dial high numbers. This was a dreadful burden – I couldn't explain it to anyone. I had to stop using the telephone. I could just about get up as high as number 5, but even that was difficult. Anything higher was impossible, and there are very few telephone numbers which don't have any digits in them higher than a 5. I could take incoming calls, but other than that I had to write letters. It was slow and inconvenient, and I knew it puzzled people to get a letter from me over some trivial matter when they would have expected me to telephone.

I couldn't even make internal calls. I had to go and see colleagues in their rooms. My office was on the third floor but I found myself going up and down the sixteen floors in our building like a yo-yo. I hardly spent any time in my own room; I was constantly rushing around. It reached a point where I had difficulty getting all my work done. I got behind with my record sheets, which meant that some evenings I had to stay in the office quite late, catching up on paperwork that I hadn't managed to complete during the day. I was working 12-hour days."

Huw paused again. For a time he seemed lost in his own thoughts; it was almost as if I wasn't in the room. When he spoke again his voice sounded as though it came from far, far away.

"It was then I had the accident."

I thought for a moment that Huw wasn't going to say any more, but then he seemed to pull himself together. He looked at me carefully.

"I'm not boring you, Gareth, am I? Shall we have a break and I'll make a cup of tea?"

"No, Huw," I said, "I'm not thirsty. Tell me what happened next."

"Well, I blame myself. I knew it was unwise to have a fire in the building. I was working late, as I'd got into the habit of doing, and I must have dozed off. I awoke to a crackling sound and a haze of smoke. It was very windy that night and perhaps a down-draught had blown some sparks into the room. My carpet was on fire and so were some papers lying on the bookcase opposite. Flames were licking along the wall. Then, as I watched, my bookcase was suddenly engulfed in flames. It was a terrible sight. I felt very frightened – the fire was past the point where I might have put it out on my own.

The smoke was so thick I could only just see across the office. I held a handkerchief to my mouth and headed for the door. I managed to cross the room and escape into the cool air of the passageway. As I closed the office door behind me, shutting out the smoke, I realised I'd have to act quickly before the fire spread to the rest of the building. As security officer I had the master key which opened the door to every room. I entered the office opposite my own and picked up the telephone to call the fire brigade.

In my panic I'd forgotten about that other business. I found I couldn't dial the number. I couldn't bring myself to dial 999. My eyes insisted on focussing on the right-hand side of the dial. Try as I might I couldn't get my fingers to shift over to the left. In desperation, I looked up the number of the local police station – 422983. No good. I tried to think of the telephone numbers of some people I knew – you can imagine, Gareth, by this stage I'd given up any thought of keeping my problems a secret – but they all contained at least one high number.

As a last resort I grabbed a telephone directory. I found a suitable number soon enough. I can remember it to this day: N J Abrahams, 73 Grove Road, telephone number 22414. I phoned the number. A lady answered. She had a very frail, old lady's voice. I asked if she would as a matter of great urgency dial 999 and call the fire brigade to the Mitchell & Morris building on Southgate Street. She asked me to repeat what I'd said. I said the same thing again, conscious as I did so that my voice was shaking. Smoke was beginning to seep under the door of the room I was in – the fire was spreading rapidly. When I'd repeated my request to the old lady, she asked me why I didn't dial the fire brigade myself. So I told her that I couldn't dial high numbers. Then I heard the phone go 'click' at the other end as the receiver was put down.

It was at that moment that I heard the sirens of the fire engines. Can you imagine my relief, Gareth? Thank goodness, I thought. The fire must be visible from the street by this time. Someone else had called the fire brigade. I made my way out of the room. I was only just in time. The walls of my own office had collapsed in flames. The fire had obviously taken a hold. It seemed unlikely that the firemen would be able to contain it.

I ran down the stairs as fast as I could and out into the street. A knot of people had gathered to look at the flames and smoke which were clearly visible at several windows on the third floor. Two fire engines had arrived and the crews were drawing out hoses and winding up their ladders. Then I heard the sound of a police siren and a police car drew up. I saw one of the small crowd of spectators detach himself from the group and go to speak to one of the officers. I saw him point at me. I knew then that I was in trouble."

"But you hadn't done anything wrong, Huw," I said. "It was an accident."

"Yes, Gareth, it was an accident, but some accidents are hard to explain. I did my best to explain it to the police. I spent the next three days at the police station, being questioned by detectives. I realised that it was my fault the fire had started. But once it started I'd done everything I could. Of course, I knew I'd lose my job. You couldn't expect the company to tolerate their safety officer breaking his own regulations and starting a fire. The fire brigade had managed to save the building, but the whole of the third floor had been destroyed. I felt very badly about it.

"But the police questioning took a turn I didn't expect. The officers asked me why I'd lit a fire in my room. I told them I'd developed a fear of central heating. I didn't make excuses – I knew I shouldn't have had a coal fire, but I explained my problem as best I could. Then they asked me why I was in the building so late. I explained that, too. I told them I was catching up on my paperwork. And then they asked why I hadn't called the fire brigade. So I told them I couldn't dial high numbers.

"I can see now it must have looked very strange to the police. They charged me with arson. When my case came to court I was asked a lot of unpleasant questions by one of the barristers. He tried to make out that I was dissatisfied with my job, that I had a grievance against the company. It was all nonsense and I told them so. I didn't like having to talk publicly about my problems, but I told the whole story, Gareth, just as I'm telling it to you now. I suppose there are some things you can't expect other people to understand."

"What did they do to you, Huw?" I asked.

"Prison, Gareth. I got seven years for arson."

I must have looked upset at that, because Huw hastened to reassure me: "Oh, it wasn't too bad. I was lucky – I got parole, so I was out in four. And as a matter of fact I didn't mind prison. You could almost say I'd come to the right place – because you know, Gareth, whatever people may say about prisons, they're not too strong on the central heating. And as for that other business, I understand it's all changed now, but when I did my stretch prisoners weren't allowed to make telephone calls."

I looked at him, open-mouthed.

"Are you better now, Huw?" I asked.

"Right as rain, Gareth," Huw replied. "I prefer not to have the central heating on, but that's just a precaution. And we have these push-button telephones now, so if I ever need to phone someone, that little weakness of mine is under control. No,

Gareth, my problems disappeared the day I went inside. It's all behind me now."

"I'm sorry, Huw," I said, "I never knew."

"Of course, you didn't. Hardly anyone knows, and between you and me, I'd rather keep it that way. You won't mention it to anyone else, will you Gareth? Not everyone's as understanding as you."

"No, of course not."

"Good boy. Not even within the family, if you'd be so kind."

Then Huw added thoughtfully, almost as an afterthought...

"Especially don't say anything to your mother. She doesn't like having a criminal for a brother-in-law."

"I won't say anything to her," I said.

"Do you promise?"

"I promise."

And that was a promise I kept.

The Amazon Forests

MY FIRST GEOGRAPHY teacher at Ardwyn Grammar School was named Hywel Goodwin. Hywel must have been about fifty-five when I knew him, but to me he appeared older. He'd lost a leg in the war, and perhaps because the artificial limb affected his mobility he had grown rather stout. Hywel also had an uncertain temper, but this was something that the pupils in his care were inclined to forgive. It was obvious that beneath the gruff exterior he was a kindly soul, and it was not difficult to imagine that his leg, or what remained of it, caused him pain. Also, Hywel in his youth had been a talented sportsman, and it cannot have been easy for him to have to live the life of a semi-invalid.

Not that Hywel gave in to his disability. His great passion was cricket, and he still played. In his day he had been a fast bowler of repute – and as far as I was concerned, having to face him in games lessons, Hywel remained a fast bowler of repute. He made no concessions to my diminutive frame or to my poor eyesight (I generally removed my glasses for games lessons, but I kept them on when I played cricket, especially when batting – less an aid to improved performance, more an unspoken plea for mercy directed at opposing fast bowlers).

It didn't work with Hywel. He would trundle up to the stumps, his face beetroot red and contorted with effort, but the awkwardness of the physical performance belied the speed and accuracy of the delivery that followed. It didn't help that I'd got it into my head that Hywel's wooden leg was not attached to the rest of him as reliably as one might wish. Accordingly, I laboured under an anxiety that the effort that went into his bowling action would lead to a rupture – in which case I imagined it would be touch and go which reached me first, Hywel's wooden leg or the ball. Either might decapitate me, and what was I to do if they arrived together?

Hywel's teaching was distinctive. He had a passion for geography and a gift for communicating the disturbing nature of his subject. Some of my teachers struck me at the time as rather grey men and women; they dictated notes from old textbooks; they made me copy out whole chapters; they blew the dust off tired teaching notes and fed them to a tired and listless audience. But Hywel was different. He'd been a tail-gunner in the war, and his approach to teaching geography bore the marks of that experience: Hywel fired facts at us as if he had so many bullets of information, he couldn't get rid of them fast enough.

And what facts they were; what leaps of understanding; what drama and significance were attached to the most outwardly prosaic topics. Hywel's lessons on economic geography were years ahead of their time. As I recall it now, we spent weeks learning about the heroin trade. I'll never forget Hywel's depiction of the illiterate Turkish peasant and the New York City junkie, the one producing and the other consuming the opium poppy. It was ten years before *The French Connection* appeared in cinemas, but Hywel was our Popeye Doyle, battling against the iniquities of the drugs trade.

Some of Hywel's lessons were almost too disturbing for an eleven year old. It was as if all his teaching was X certificate; there was no watered-down version for the junior forms. I can remember when he taught us about the Panama Canal; Hywel had thirty eleven year olds wide-eyed with wonder as he told us of the fantastic cost in lives and money of forcing the knife-cut of the Panama Canal through ninety miles of mountains to link the Pacific and Atlantic oceans. Then he said: "Of course, they'll never build another one. The Pacific is two inches higher than the Atlantic – it wouldn't be worth the risk."

Hywel said it had something to do with the earth spinning on its axis and this affecting the gravitational pull – or perhaps it was the gravitational pull affecting the earth spinning on its axis, I'm not entirely sure. Whichever way round it was, it was a frightening thought. Even two inches off the top of the Pacific Ocean must be a lot of water. I imagined some unwary Central American engineer, not possessed of Hywel's encyclopaedic knowledge of oceans, attempting to cut a second Panama Canal and being met with a wall of water, high as a mountain, as the extra two inches off the top of the Pacific came thundering down on him.

When I mentioned this to my father he wasn't as impressed as I had been. Dad knew Hywel because they belonged to the same bowling club.

"What does Hywel Goodwin think he's talking about?" he said to me. "Pacific two inches higher than the Atlantic, indeed. He's measured it, has he? I bet he's never been west of Fishguard all his life."

That wasn't true about Hywel not having been further west than Fishguard, as dad well knew, but I found it difficult to argue with my father. I was sure Hywel was right, even if I had to admit that it was a difficult thing to prove. I can still remember dad's final words on the subject:

"Ask Hywel," he said, "if he's heard of Cape Horn. That's where the Pacific and Atlantic oceans meet. I know it's rough, but I've never heard of a waterfall. Ask him if there's a notice to sailors saying 'mind the step'."

As I say, I found it difficult to argue with my father, but Hywel's lessons didn't lose their appeal for me. They mostly revolved around the elemental forces of nature – water being his favourite, as having the greatest potential for calamity.

Once, when he was teaching us about the great Russian plains, which he told us were called the steppes, he mentioned that the Russian government had formulated a plan to divert one of the country's biggest rivers – the Dvina I think it was – so that instead of flowing north into the Arctic Ocean, it would flow due south into the Black Sea.

"Do you know what effect that would have?" Hywel asked us. Of course none of us knew.

Hywel paused dramatically. "It would turn Iceland into a frozen desert," he said.

Nobody said anything. I thought Iceland already was a frozen desert, but I wasn't going to say that to Hywel. We waited for him to continue.

"The Dvina brings warm water from the central plains of Russia into the northern oceans," he went on. "If you cut off that supply of water like a tap…" (Hywel gave a vicious twist to his wrist like someone attempting to turn off a tap with a faulty washer) "the temperature of the Arctic Ocean will fall, and the seas as far south as Iceland will be frozen over."

I imagined some Russian peasant, working his patch of land on the steppes, somewhere near the source of the Dvina. One day he might decide to alter the course of the stream that welled up outside his hut. He'd get a few boulders and change the direction of flow, so that the stream ran south, instead of north as it had done for centuries past. And all of Iceland would be frozen over. It made me go cold just to think about it, and I didn't even live in Iceland.

Such knowledge was quite a burden for an eleven year old. I started to worry about the Severn and the Wye, both of which rise in the Cambrian Mountains north-east of Aberystwyth. What would happen if some English tourist were maliciously to divert those great rivers so that they flowed, not leisurely eastwards to the Bristol Channel, but headlong due west down the ten miles of the Rheidol valley into Aberystwyth? Would the whole town be wiped out? Only Hywel knew the answer, but I was afraid to ask him.

Hywel retired at the end of my second year in Ardwyn, but he retained to the end his ability to disturb his young audience. His final subject was Brazil. He told us about the great Amazon river and how many gallons of water flowed down the Amazon to the sea; I forget how many gallons it was, and I'm not sure if the figure Hywel gave us was per day or per second, but I understood that the Amazon was an enormous river, much bigger than any of ours.

Then Hywel told us about the Amazon rainforest. He said that the Amazon was the greatest forest in the world. I suppose he told us how many trees there were, but I've forgotten that as well. Then Hywel said that the world was dependent on the Amazon forest for its oxygen supply; if it weren't for the Amazon, we wouldn't be able to breathe. "Oh, and by the way," he said, "they're chopping it down."

That was Hywel's final lesson to our class. I was very sad that he was leaving. There were so many questions left unanswered. How quickly were they chopping down the Amazon? When would we run out of oxygen? Should we plant more trees, or have fewer babies? What had the Russians decided to do about the Dvina? Did the Panamanian government know the height of the Pacific Ocean?

A few days later dad caught me holding my breath, so I had to tell him about the Amazon, and how they were chopping it down.

"Wait till I see Hywel Goodwin," he said. "Pure sensationalism, that's what that is. God almighty would have more sense than to rely on trees alone to produce oxygen; grass could do the job just as well."

I never did find out whether grass could produce oxygen, as

my father said it could. It didn't seem likely somehow. Hywel Goodwin had conjured up a world that was dependent upon a fine balance of cataclysmic forces. Every tree and river was significant, with disaster lurking around the next bend or boulder. It was a disturbing vision for impressionable young minds, but then Hywel Goodwin was a disturbing man.

Aberystwyth Boy

My brother Owen was an unlikely sporting hero. This was not by reason of any lack of natural sporting talent – it wasn't easy to determine the extent of Owen's athletic abilities because he displayed little interest in conventional sporting pursuits. He made no effort to exert himself in weekly games lessons, and whilst I was desperate to earn a place in school rugby teams for my age group, Owen appeared indifferent. The one thing you could say for Owen was that he seemed impervious to pain. If there was a tackle to be attempted, Owen would fling himself at the opposing player, head first. He never mastered the technique of aiming slightly to one side of an onrushing opponent, so that his shoulder took the force of the blow. Owen favoured the full-frontal assault, with consequences that were predictable and, you would have thought, extremely painful. It was a style of tackling that is familiar to devotees of American football, where the players wear helmets. Owen had no such protection, and in consequence he was both admired and feared by his classmates, most of whom had fallen victim at one time or another to Owen's kamikaze assaults.

This did not threaten Owen's popularity with his peers. He was in all other respects the most peaceable of boys, and his ferocious tackling was a reflection of his idiosyncratic nature rather than a strongly competitive spirit. Whatever sporting success Owen achieved was accidental, and all the more notable for its appearing so unlikely. More typically, Owen's sporting endeavours ended in failure, but even his failures tended to be distinctive, and therefore memorable. For example, who could forget Owen's attempt to throw the javelin on school sports day, and the consternation around the long jump pit as Owen's ill-directed missile thudded into the sand? Not those long jumpers, and certainly not 'Biff' Rowlands, our History teacher at the time, who was chief long jump judge for the day. Biff was stood in the sand pit at the time, and Owen's javelin missed him by inches. Many years later I encountered Biff on the promenade in Aberystwyth. "Your brother tried to kill me," he said.

An equally strong impression was created by Owen's participation in the annual school boxing tournament. Old Llew – Mr Llewelyn, our headmaster – believed that boxing helped develop moral fibre. Accordingly, once a year he took it upon himself to organise an inter-house boxing competition. It so happened that Owen's first year in Ardwyn was the last year in which the boxing tournament was held. It was becoming increasingly difficult to find boys who were willing to participate. Most of us had a shrewd idea of our pugilistic limitations – I know I did. We were also well aware that some boys in the school were natural hard cases who relished an opportunity to use their fists. The three Morris brothers, for example, were enthusiastic fighters in or out of the ring; they signed up for boxing as a matter of course. The rest of us did not feel the same compulsion. I occasionally got into fights, and I nearly always lost. I saw no good reason why I should submit to being beaten up officially, as well as unofficially.

The school house to which Owen and I belonged was Gwynedd, and Gwynedd did not contain many hard cases. Accordingly, it was not easy for the games teachers to recruit representatives for the boxing tournament. They had to find boxers in six weight categories, the lightest being for boys weighing under six stone, this being Owen's weight at the time. Owen had no interest in boxing, and nor did most of the other boys in his class, but Llew insisted that all the weight categories be filled. So it transpired that Owen, with his characteristic mix of innocence and foolhardiness, volunteered to represent Gwynedd in the under six stone category in that year's school boxing tournament. I am fairly certain that Owen had never hit anyone in his life. He'd certainly never strapped on boxing gloves or entered a boxing ring.

Whilst Llew thought it character-building for the boys in his charge to be dragooned into entering a boxing tournament, he did not consider it his responsibility to avoid gross mismatches, or to counter these by way of prior instruction. So Owen's first experience of boxing came in the tournament itself. His scheduled opponent was Freddie Morris. Freddie was in Owen's class, but there any similarity ended. Anyone who looked for a moment into young Freddie's pale blue eyes would have been left in no doubt that he was the hardest of hard nuts. He did not go out of his way to advertise this – none of the Morris boys did; Freddie's cool, unflinching gaze was more than sufficient. And yet Freddie was a friend of Owen's. Some of us took comfort from this – surely Freddie would not want to hurt Owen? And to his considerable credit, that was indeed Freddie's view of the matter. He had been looking forward to the tournament, and to bashing someone's brains in, but Freddie was dismayed to discover that it was Owen's brains he was meant to bash.

On the morning of the boxing tournament I helped Owen lace up his boxing gloves, which he'd never seen before. They were enormous things, extending right up Owen's arms to the elbow. There was an intricate scheme of laces by which the gloves were to be attached to Owen's puny forearms. The gloves were exceedingly heavy, deliberately so I suppose, in order to prevent inexperienced fighters inflicting significant damage upon one another. Owen was barely able to lift his hands to the level of his chin.

"OK, Owen?" I enquired.

"These are heavy," was all he said.

The fight did not last long. Owen and Freddie advanced to the centre of the ring. There was a pause, with Freddie plainly uncertain what to do. Then Owen pulled back his right arm, half hidden within its enormous boxing glove, in anticipation of delivering a telling blow. As he wound himself up to deliver this punch, Freddie tapped Owen lightly on the nose. Owen staggered backwards. Undaunted, he advanced once more and prepared to deliver a second haymaker. As before, Freddie tapped Owen on the nose, and Owen's haymaker never arrived.

And so the 'fight' continued. Freddie was determined not to hurt Owen, and so restricted himself to delivering light taps to the end of Owen's nose. Owen meanwhile was doing his level best – if not to hurt, then at least to hit Freddie – but his punches kept being interrupted by Freddie's practised jab, which whenever Owen approached within a few feet snaked out and tapped Owen on the nose. Owen's haymaker was forever on the verge of being delivered, but it never arrived. Even when Owen managed to complete the roundhouse swing that was his favoured method, his boxing glove made such weary progress towards its intended target that by the time it arrived Freddie had long since departed the spot at which Owen had been aiming.

After two minutes of this, the referee, old Chadwick, signalled that the contest was at an end. Owen's nose looked a bit inflamed, but other than that he was unharmed. "Bloodied but unbowed, eh Owen?" said Chadwick. Owen was disinclined to discuss the matter. I could tell he was disappointed. "Gloves too heavy," was all he said.

I understand that in later years Freddie Morris became an accomplished amateur boxer. There was even talk of his following his older brother into the professional ranks, but those who knew Freddie said he lacked the necessary killer instinct. Maybe it was that fight with Owen that did it. I've sometimes wondered if Owen didn't ruin Freddie's boxing career.

Owen continued to explore a range of sporting interests, without threatening to distinguish himself in any of them. What marked Owen out from the rest of us was a dogged determination to follow his own path. This was demonstrated most powerfully by his decision, aged thirteen, to enter the Ardwyn school cycle race. This was an annual event dominated by those pupils who were enthusiastic members of Ystwyth Wheelers, the cycling club in the town. They were often to be seen out on their training rides, riding in formation on their streamlined racing machines. It was an impressive sight, far removed from the kind of cycling that Owen or I attempted.

For we too had bikes, but ours were not of the racing variety. Dad had purchased them for us second-hand, and we used them for getting about the town. They were thick-wheeled and heavy-framed, with gears which often jammed, forcing us to dismount on steep inclines. Owen's bike had an additional problem in that his chain would periodically detach from the chain wheel, necessitating impromptu repairs which left Owen oil-spattered and enraged. Nonetheless Owen was proud of his bike and for the most part he enjoyed riding it.

It was a surprise to me that Owen wished to enter a race for which he had not trained, and for which he was so poorly equipped. I know others took the same view. By far the best cyclist in Ardwyn was Rob Wills, a stick-thin young man whose awkward frame and angular gait were transformed once in the saddle. Rob spent all his free time pursuing his hobby, which he viewed with the utmost seriousness. The sight of Owen lining up at the school gates with his sturdy sit-up-and-beg machine discomfited Rob.

"You're not going to ride that, are you?" he enquired.

"Why not?" Owen replied.

"It's a tough route," Rob observed mildly, "and that's a heavy bike."

"I know," said Owen. "I'm used to it."

The course to be followed took the riders from the school gates, out onto the A44 heading due east from Aberystwyth in the direction of the village of Ponterwyd. The first five miles were relatively flat, but from Capel Bangor onwards the road tilted sharply uphill, with five miles of unremitting climbing into the lower slopes of the Cambrian Mountains. There was then a two-mile downhill stretch into Ponterwyd, where the cyclists were directed to turn right, leaving the A44 to follow the mountain road to Devil's Bridge. Once having reached Devil's Bridge there would be some respite, with the twelve miles from Devil's Bridge back to Aberystwyth being for the most part only mildly undulating, concluding with a downhill finish into the town.

It was a circuit well known to Rob Wills and the other members of Ystwyth Wheelers. Other than the first few miles, it would be a new experience for Owen. He and I had on a few occasions cycled out to Capel Bangor, where we had drunk dandelion and burdock and eaten doughnuts beside the Rheidol river, but Owen had never cycled into the mountains.

The fifteen cyclists who had volunteered for the race were sent on their way at 9.30 in the morning. Owen was disconcerted to observe that the other fourteen all disappeared from view around the first corner even as he was taking his first few pedal strokes. It hadn't occurred to him before what a gulf there was between cycling as a competitive sport and his own unhurried perambulations. Owen had imagined that he would have company for at least part of the route. Now he was facing the fact that for the entire distance of the race he would be cycling alone.

Nonetheless, Owen pressed on. He hadn't expected to win

the race, but he had hoped not to finish last. Now he revised his expectations. He was grimly determined to complete the course, and what's more to do so in a time and in a manner that – given the limitations of his equipment – would be no disgrace. For the next few miles Owen cycled along with a feeling of relative serenity. His bike was behaving itself, and the terrain was not too demanding. By 10.15 he had reached Capel Bangor. Rob Wills meanwhile had slalomed up the mountain roads and was approaching Ponterwyd. Even on the uphill stretches of the course he was travelling at twice Owen's speed.

It was once past Capel Bangor that Owen's difficulties began. That was where the serious climbing started, and the additional pressure on the pedals led to Owen's bicycle chain – a fragile instrument at the best of times – becoming unhitched from its wheel. So Owen found himself having to effect repairs. He was also becoming tired. He had never previously attempted to propel his bike up these inclines, and there were times when he had to walk. In truth, walking hardly slowed him down, his progress whilst in the saddle having become so painfully slow.

It took Owen the best part of an hour to negotiate those five miles, but eventually he hauled himself up the final long drag at the head of the Rheidol valley and was able to look down the way he had come. The Rheidol valley viewed from the vantage point of the Nantyrarian pass has an ethereal beauty, but this barely registered with Owen. He grunted to himself with satisfaction at what he had accomplished. Suitably encouraged, he embarked on the downhill run to Ponterwyd. Rob Wills was at that moment riding serenely through the gates of Ardwyn. He promptly turned around and rode back down the course towards Llanbadarn with a view to encouraging his fellow riders.

Owen meanwhile pressed on, enjoying the feel of the wind on his cheeks as he freewheeled down the slope into Ponterwyd. This was where the race route diverted from the A44, to follow the mountain road to Devil's Bridge. And here it was that things began to go badly wrong for Owen. He had not familiarised himself with the route, imagining either that he would be in the company of other cyclists or that there would be marshals at the roadside who would give directions. But Owen was on his own and there were no marshals. Had he not been so tired, he might have remembered that he was required to turn right in Ponterwyd, but in his exhausted state Owen was no longer thinking clearly. He continued along the A44 in the direction of Llangurig.

No longer on the race route, Owen now faced a further gruelling uphill stretch. There would be no respite for the next five miles as the A44 snaked upwards towards Eisteddfa Gurig. Owen didn't know it, but he was heading into the heart of the Cambrian Mountains, with the mighty Plynlimon off to his left. The watershed, beyond which the rivers Wye and Severn rise and head eastwards, was still several miles distant.

Owen at this point was facing another problem: he was becoming desperately thirsty. On one particularly steep incline he abandoned his bike and clambered down a bank to scoop up water from a stream. It offered him little respite. He had promised himself he would cycle all the way, but he hadn't counted on all these miles uphill. Nonetheless, he pressed on. Three and a half hours after leaving the gates of Ardwyn, he arrived at Eisteddfa Gurig. Eisteddfa Gurig is only a bridge over a stream, and the significance of the mountain watershed was lost on Owen, but he noted dully that the road was no longer climbing, and he felt relieved at that.

By this time all the other cyclists had returned to Ardwyn. As I waited at the school gates I was becoming concerned that there was as yet no sign of Owen. Rob Wills said he would go to look for him, cycling round the course in the reverse direction. It was very nice of Rob, and for a time I felt my anxieties ease.

But then a thought struck me, and I went in search of Chadwick, the games teacher. I told him I wasn't sure Owen knew the race route. Chadwick said that if Rob Wills didn't return with Owen within the next hour, he'd organise a proper search.

It is eight miles from Eisteddfa Gurig to Llangurig, and although the road is undulating, it is mostly downhill. In normal circumstances Owen would have managed it comfortably, but by this stage he was terribly tired. Cars were passing frequently, but there was no-one by the roadside with whom Owen might have checked the route. So he kept pedalling. There were frequent downhill stretches, but these were punctuated by vicious inclines which Owen could feel were draining him of the last of his strength.

It was half-past two when Owen drifted down the final slope into Llangurig. The village appeared deserted but there was a petrol station by the roadside, and Owen stopped beside it. He hobbled in the direction of the office, noting with interest that his legs no longer obeyed his brain's commands. Owen had no money, but the lady minding the till directed him to the toilet, where he drank greedily from the cold tap.

Owen drank and drank, and as he did so he caught sight of himself in the mirror. He was shocked to see how tired and bedraggled he looked. His face was covered with grime from his chain wheel, but Owen was too tired to wipe it off. He drank some more, and then he went back to the office. He asked the lady how far it was to Devil's Bridge. She'd heard of Devil's Bridge, she told him, but she didn't know where it was. She was new to the area, she explained.

"Have you any money?" she asked Owen.

Owen shook his head.

"Would you like an ice cream?"

Owen didn't feel comfortable about accepting this gift, but hunger was gnawing at his stomach.

"Thank you," he said.

"Perhaps if you ask at Rhayader," the lady suggested, "someone may be able to help you there."

"Which way is Rhayader?" Owen asked.

"Keep right at the fork," she told him.

Owen finished his ice cream. He didn't know what to do for the best, and in his befuddled state he struggled to formulate a plan. If he'd known that he had just traversed the Cambrian Mountains he might have taken some pride in his achievement, but Owen's command of local geography was limited. He only knew that he was lost. Still, he wanted to finish the race. He saw no alternative other than to carry on to Rhayader, as the lady suggested. Perhaps someone there would be able to help him.

The entrance to Ardwyn Grammar School is normally deserted at 4.30 in the afternoon, staff and pupils having departed for the day. But on the day of the school cycle race there was unaccustomed activity and hubbub. Dad had arrived, accompanied by my Uncle Huw, and there were two police cars in attendance. There were also ten members of Ystwyth Wheelers sitting astride their bikes. They had offered their services to help in the search for Owen. Llew was also there, looking very stern as he talked to Chadwick and other senior members of staff.

Dad was looking white and strained. I watched as he spoke to the two police officers. He called me over. "Did Owen say anything to you?" dad asked me. I shook my head. Owen and I hadn't discussed the race. There were things I might have said that would have helped, but I didn't know how to formulate them. I knew Owen better than anyone, but I couldn't begin to work out where he might have got to. "His bike may have packed up," was the only suggestion I could offer.

Dad and the police officers were trying to formulate a plan. "We've got two hours," one of the policemen was saying, "it'll be dark by then." One of the officers had a map, and he was drawing lines on it, working out which roads the volunteer helpers should cover. He consulted the cyclists, and then everyone disappeared, each having been assigned a route. Dad asked me if I wanted to come with him and Huw, but I said that I preferred to stay by the school gates. I knew by this stage it was very unlikely that Owen would complete the course, but I couldn't get it out of my head that he would find his way back to Ardwyn. That's what I'd wanted to explain to the policemen, but I couldn't find the words: no-one who didn't know Owen could fully appreciate his doggedness, or his stubbornness in the face of adversity.

I stayed at the school gates until six o'clock, by which time it was beginning to get dark. I knew that Owen had no lights on his bike, and it was hard to believe that even he would continue riding in the dark. Mam was sitting in the house on her own when I got home. She looked at me hopefully as I walked in, and I wished with all my heart I had some good news to tell her. Dad and Huw returned a few minutes later. Huw shook his head at me, while dad went to comfort my mother.

*

The phone call came at eight o'clock. It was dad who answered. A man's voice asked if he was Mr Jenkins, and dad said he was. Then the man said: "I've just been talking to your son."

"Where are you?" dad asked.

"I farm in the Elan valley," the man replied.

"Your boy came through here a few minutes ago. I offered to take him in, but he said he had to get to Aberystwyth. I told him he's not going to manage that tonight."

"Thank you," dad said. "Would you mind telling me precisely where you are?"

Leaving mam to make the necessary phone calls, dad, Huw and I headed off into the night. It took dad over an hour to drive the thirty-five miles to Rhayader. He drove in silence, with each one of us lost in our own thoughts. At Rhayader dad took the right turn and headed into the Elan valley. Owen's route from that point, had he managed to find his way, would have involved a further crossing of the Cambrian Mountains, this time on unlit mountain roads. It's doubtful he would have survived it.

Dad drove carefully along the single-track road, avoiding the sheep that wandered across our path. There was no moon – the night was pitch-black. There were places where the road forked and I wouldn't have known the way, but dad made his choice confidently. He drove on, none of us uttering a word. After about twenty minutes I thought I could discern an expanse of water to our left, but it was difficult to tell – the car headlights only pierced the gloom for the few yards immediately ahead of us. Then we began to climb steeply and dad had to engage first gear. The road surface was pitted and the car lurched between the potholes. Our headlights bounced off the road surface as we climbed steadily, our eyes glued to the road ahead.

After about ten minutes of steady climbing there was a flatter stretch, and as we eased our way along it I thought I saw a dark shape by the roadside, some fifty yards ahead of us. Dad drove carefully up to this dark splodge, and as the car headlights picked him out we could see it was Owen, crouched over his bike. He was trying to fix his chain. Dad turned off the engine and Owen peered back at us. I think he was dazzled by the car headlights – he gave no sign he knew it was us. He turned again to his chain, assisted now by the beam of light from dad's headlights.

"Owen!" dad yelled, "get in the car!"

Owen stared at the car headlights as if mesmerised.

"What about my bike?" he called.

"Leave the bloody bike!"

It wasn't like dad to swear. It was a sign of the strain he'd been under.

Dad had great difficulty in turning the car round – the road was so narrow, there was a risk of it becoming trapped in the bog that lay either side of us – but eventually he managed it. I wanted to ask Owen what had happened, but when I looked at him I could see he was too exhausted to speak. His face was a mask of grime and his cheeks were hollow. Within a few seconds of getting in the car he had fallen asleep in the seat beside me.

We never recovered Owen's bike, and to the best of my knowledge that was Owen's last cycle ride. He stayed in bed for most of the following day, and when he did get up he had to cling to the furniture for support. It was several days before Owen was anything like his normal self.

The story of Owen's cycle ride was told and re-told, doubtless with some embellishment, and for a while it gave Owen a measure of local celebrity. But he was not a boy who enjoyed the limelight. Anyway, his cycle ride was not a cause of much satisfaction to him. Owen did not relish his reputation for eccentricity. He would have preferred a more straightforward sporting achievement.

Others, however, saw much to admire in Owen's cycle ride. Rob Wills was one who made no secret of his respect for Owen. I used to see the two of them chatting together. It was Rob who ensured that Owen's ride received modest official acknowledgement. In that year's *Ardwynian* magazine, in the section devoted to sporting success, the result of the school cycle race appeared as follows.

ANNUAL SCHOOL CYCLE RACE

Short course:
1st Rob Wills: 1 hour, 34 mins, 17 seconds
2nd Alun Thomas: 1 hour, 48 mins, 36 seconds
3rd Geoff Thomas: 1 hour, 55 mins, 8 seconds

Long course:
Owen Jenkins

I brought the magazine home to show to our dad. He read the cycle race result, then glanced at Owen, standing beside me.

"What do you think, Owen?" he enquired. "I see they didn't give your time."

"They couldn't, could they?" Owen replied. "I didn't finish."

Owen liked to act the curmudgeon, but dad and I both noticed that he kept his copy of that school magazine.

Gareth Makes his Name

WHEN I WAS a teenager in Aberystwyth I suffered from the usual teenage afflictions. In my case these including spots, chronic shyness, and unrequited love. I also had a couple of additional problems all to myself: I was the smallest boy in my class – even aged fifteen I found it impossible to get into 'X' films; and secondly, I had the same name as the outstanding Welsh rugby player of the day. That may not sound a bad thing, and as a matter of fact I wasn't a bad rugby player myself, but I could have done without the comparisons. Gareth Jenkins – which is also my name – was the Welsh outside-half. They used to call him 'Jinks' because of his name and because of his sidestep. They used to call me 'Jinks' too at school, but I was under seven stone, and by the time I reached the fifth form I couldn't see the ball without my glasses.

When I was fifteen, going on sixteen, what I wanted most in all the world was a girlfriend. But the chances of my getting one – of my being able, if I wanted, to kiss a girl – seemed impossibly remote. This was despite the fact that I knew, deep inside myself, that some girls quite liked me. They smiled at me, anyway; and I suppose, without being immodest, that in light of knowledge gained over the years some girls would have quite liked me to ask them out. But could I bring myself to say the necessary words? No I could not. It's easy to look back on it now and say to myself – 'How could I have been such a clot?' – but at the time it wasn't so easy.

It didn't help that my brother Owen was practically drowning in female attention. He didn't do anything to make this happen – Owen appeared sublimely indifferent to the adoration he inspired amongst the girls in his class – but there was no getting away from the fact that young women of Owen's acquaintance saw something in him they thought they could work on. Even Fabienne, the young French girl who arrived one summer to stay with the Roberts family who lived in the house immediately behind ours – a family that included two boys of roughly Owen's and my age – had just one chance encounter with Owen at our front gate and was immediately smitten. This was an inconvenient passion, since the two Roberts boys might reasonably have considered themselves first in line, but Fabienne was not deterred. She devised a system that involved her hanging a pink sponge bag on the latch of her bedroom window whenever she was free to rendezvous with Owen. Owen did not consider it worth his while to spend his days gazing up at Fabienne's bedroom window, so it was left to our mother, stationed in the kitchen, to keep a lookout. This she did with great enthusiasm. "Owen!" mam would cry, "sponge bag!" And off Owen would trot.

What wouldn't I have given to inspire such devotion. But whereas Owen was relaxed and totally unselfconscious in the company of girls of his own age, I was a bundle of nerves. Naturally the other boys in my class helped me out as much as they could by making confidence-boosting remarks. For example, every time a particularly tall girl would walk by, someone would shout, "Here's one for you, Jinks." It would have put anyone off their stroke.

My name was a problem, too. You can imagine how the other boys used to harp on about it, implying that they were in the presence of greatness. I got used to that, but something happened in the winter of my fifth form year that made me wish with all my heart that I wasn't named Gareth Jenkins. It was a boy called Emyr Humphries who was the cause of it all. Emyr was the kind of boy who got into a lot of trouble at school, but he was very popular and I think even the teachers liked him as long as he wasn't in their class. It was Emyr who tripped on the top step and fell flat on his face when he went up on to the stage to collect his 'O' level certificate at school assembly. I can still recall the look of disgust on old Llew's face as he waited for Emyr to haul himself to his feet whilst the whole school erupted. Emyr only got one 'O' level, but we all remembered it.

One January evening Emyr and I were sitting in a café in Aberystwyth called The Milk Bar. It was the week of the first rugby international of the season which that year was between Wales and Scotland at Cardiff Arms Park. Emyr and I had tickets for the game. As we sat there, discussing the prospects for Saturday, two girls I'd never seen before walked into The Milk Bar and sat down. Left to my own devices I would have ignored them, but that wasn't Emyr's way. "Come on," he said to me, "let's have a word." No sooner had he said this than Emyr was on his way to where the girls were sitting. I followed, some way behind and with a distracted air that I hoped conveyed the message that this was entirely Emyr's idea and that I would be perfectly happy to go straight back to where I'd come from.

But that wasn't necessary. The girls seemed pleased to talk to us – or at least, to Emyr. Their names were Linda and Janet and they were sisters. They'd come from London to Aberystwyth with their parents. I wanted to ask why anyone would move to Aberystwyth in the middle of winter, but I didn't know if it was the right thing to say, so I kept quiet. Anyway, Emyr did enough talking for both of us. He was chatting away and suddenly I heard him say: "Now then girls, let me introduce you to my friend Gareth, sitting here so modest and quiet. No-one would think he's a famous rugby player. Gareth plays outside-half for Wales."

I expected the girls to laugh, but all that happened was that Linda, the taller one who was sitting opposite Emyr, said, "What's outside-half?"

"The one who gets the ball from the scrum-half," I said. They were the first words I'd spoken. Not very helpful, I can see now. I should have said: "Emyr, don't be ridiculous; I'm fifteen years old and I haven't even played for the school first team." But for whatever reason, I didn't. Emyr had taken over. "He's playing for Wales against Scotland on Saturday," he continued. "We're all going to Cardiff Arms Park to watch."

"Shut up, Emyr," I said. Janet, the younger-looking one of the two girls, looked at me in a thoughtful, serious way. "Don't mind him," she said. I'd never had much to do with girls and I wasn't used to them talking to me, but Janet spoke softly, and she was more friendly than frightening. I found myself wishing I wasn't with Emyr. I decided that if Janet and her sister wanted to believe that I played for Wales, they could believe it as far as I was concerned. I hadn't said anything that wasn't true. Emyr was already talking about something else.

When Janet and Linda got up to leave, Janet said to me: "Will you be here tomorrow?"

"Er… yes, I think so," I said.

"What time?"

"About seven, I think."

"Shall I see you then?"

"All right."

It was my first date if you want to know, although I wouldn't have admitted that to anyone at the time. I hadn't done anything to engineer it, and it seemed to me to be a sort of miracle.

I saw Janet twice more that week. I kept out of Emyr's way;

I didn't know whether to be pleased or angry with him about that stupid story. I never mentioned it to Janet and she showed no inclination to talk about it. I liked her a lot. I suppose she knew I wasn't really a famous rugby player, but I wasn't going to bring up the subject. She didn't seem to be interested in rugby, although it's obvious that it would make a difference to a girl if she thought you played for Wales.

That Friday evening I was walking Janet home when we saw Emyr approaching. "Hey, Jinks boy!" he shouted. "Good luck for tomorrow!"

"Thanks," I said. Janet ignored him.

On the Saturday Emyr and I travelled together to Cardiff to watch the game. It was very exciting, what I could see of it. Wales beat Scotland quite easily in the end. Gareth Jenkins was outstanding, scoring one try and kicking three penalties. I wished I could be playing for Wales like that, but as it was it made me feel a bit uncomfortable – him playing so well and supposed to be me. Or me supposed to be him. It even affected my enjoyment of the game. It was quite late when we arrived back in Aberystwyth, but we drove straight round to Emyr's house. He'd arranged a little party to celebrate the Welsh victory – Emyr was always the optimist, but it's true Wales had a very good side that year. Janet had told me she hoped to come to Emyr's party. I was looking forward to seeing her, but I was worried about Emyr and what further nonsense he might be planning.

When I got to Emyr's house everyone was talking about the game. I stayed out of the way as much I could, talking to Janet. Every now and then Emyr would sidle up to us and make some reference to my performance.

"Jinks," he would say, "you were magnificent. Just talk us through that try again, boy."

"No thanks," I said.

I was glad that Janet didn't seem interested in the game. I

suppose I'd have been a bit upset if I'd been the real Gareth Jenkins, but since I wasn't, it didn't matter.

Then Emyr did something that even now I find it hard to forgive him for; I get embarrassed just thinking about it. He turned on the radio that was in the room and tuned it to the Home Service. The Welsh sports programme *Sports Review* was on and the experts were discussing the Wales/Scotland game. I looked across at Emyr and signalled to him to turn the radio off, but it was difficult to say much with Janet standing next to me. Anyway, Emyr pretended not to notice. He turned the volume up so that both Janet and I could hear what was being said.

Just at that moment the chairman of the panel of experts could be heard saying: "We're delighted to have the opportunity of a few words with the Welsh hero of the afternoon, Gareth Jenkins."

"Hey Jinks!" said Emyr. "Listen to yourself here, boy."

Very funny. I had a kind of sick, empty feeling in my stomach, like you do when you've fallen over and hurt yourself very badly. I looked at Janet.

"I suppose they record these interviews after the game," was what she actually said.

"Yes," I said, "that's what they usually do."

Recorded? Of course it was recorded. The question of who exactly had been recorded slipped by without needing to be addressed. The crisis was over as quickly as it had begun. For the first time that evening, I could relax.

Janet and I never mentioned rugby again. Her family only stayed in Aberystwyth for a few months. They left that spring, taking Janet with them. I haven't seen her for many years, but she was my first girlfriend and very important to me. She taught me how wise some girls are.

Uncle Huw

As you'll know by now, Uncle Huw was my father's brother, and he lived on his own in a small cottage on the edge of Bow Street, just outside Aberystwyth. When Owen and I were growing up we spent a lot of time with Huw. We used to cycle the three miles to his home on most weekends, and sometimes in the week as well.

"It does my heart good to see you, boys," Huw would say as he'd rush to open the drawer of an old cupboard behind his chair where he kept the sweets and cakes that he used to give us. It was dark and quite dirty inside Huw's cottage but we didn't mind that. He had a lot of funny stories that he used to tell us, and he'd make jokes, ever so quick, in reply to things we said. But if I ever told my mother that I'd been to visit Huw, she would look cross and say something like: "You'll grow to be like him, spending all your time out there. One in the family's enough to be wasting his life away." My mother didn't have a lot of time for Huw. She never used to visit him, as far as I could tell.

Owen and I would watch television with Huw on Saturday afternoons. As we watched he'd bring us cups of tea, always with a chocolate biscuit in the saucer. Huw used to pour a measure of whisky into his own tea cup. "Just a drop," he'd say, "to keep me from nodding off." I don't know if Huw would have nodded off without his whisky, but I suppose it was quite likely because even with the whisky he used to nod off quite a bit.

The programme we watched together was *Grandstand*. We mostly watched the horse racing. That's when I first realised that not only was Huw a very funny man, he was a very wise one as well.

"Boys," he'd say to us, "don't you ever be gamblers. The bookies always win in the end. I'll show you if you like."

Then Huw would demonstrate to us how the bookies always won in the end. "I'll be the bookmaker," he'd say, "and you have a bet with me."

So we started to place a few bets with Huw. Owen and I would each put a shilling on some horse we'd picked out on the television. Sometimes our horse would win and Huw would pay us the money he owed us according to the odds on the television. More often than not our horse would lose and then Huw would keep the two shillings that we'd wagered with him.

It wasn't long before Huw suggested that rather than place our bets with him, we might as well wager a few shillings at the local betting shop. Owen was reluctant, but Huw and I began to bet small sums of money with Coral, the betting shop newly opened in the town. I'd give Huw a few shillings and each Saturday morning he'd come into Aberystwyth and place bets on the horses we fancied. I would just bet on one or two horses, but Huw's favourite bet was a 'yankee', which was a multiple bet on several horses. He explained to me that were all your horses to win, you could win a considerable sum from a relatively small stake.

Then on Saturday afternoons, Huw and I would watch racing on the television together, and the following Monday Huw would collect our winnings, if there were any. I don't believe his yankee ever came up. Some Saturdays all our horses would lose and Huw would say to me, "There you are, Gareth, what did I tell you? The bookies always win in the end."

I never doubted that the reason Huw backed horses was to prove to Owen and me that gambling was a mug's game. Not that Owen needed much convincing. He was never an enthusiastic gambler and he declined to participate in the betting shop venture. "I'm broke as it is," he said to me; "why do I need to be any broker?"

In time I too found other things to do with my Saturday afternoons and my visits to see Huw became less frequent. I still had the occasional bet, but my interest in horse racing had begun to wane. It just showed how wise Huw was to have taken the trouble to demonstrate to Owen and me that gambling didn't pay.

But even as my own interest in horse racing was petering out, I couldn't help noticing that Huw no longer followed his own advice. Even without my involvement he continued to place bets with Coral, and I don't think it was only on Saturdays. I didn't tell my parents this. As I've said, my mother was inclined to be critical of Huw.

I can still remember the last race that Huw and I watched together. It was the 1963 Grand National, and Huw had made a special point of asking me to go out to Bow Street that Saturday so we could watch the big race together. He had spent some time analysing the form of all the horses in the race, and was convinced he had a winning strategy.

Huw explained to me that in order to do well in the National, a horse needed to have previous experience of the Aintree fences, and preferably to have actually won the big race. There were forty-seven runners in that year's field. They included three previous winners, plus a few other strongly-fancied contenders. Huw was sure that the winner was going to come from one of eight horses that he had identified. He had bet on all eight. He said that one of those eight horses was bound to win, so he might as well back them all. That way he ensured a modest profit.

Huw's enthusiasm was infectious, and I found myself looking forward to that year's Grand National as I had to no other race. When Saturday came, Huw and I shared in the excitement of the build-up, and then we watched the big race together as, one by one, Huw's selections fell by the wayside. I had expected his horses to pull away from the remainder of the field quite easily, but the race did not go according to Huw's expectations. One of his horses fell at the very first fence. Huw let out a small groan. Another got rid of his rider by coming to a sudden stop just when his jockey was expecting him to jump an enormous fence called The Chair. The jockey cleared The Chair without difficulty, but his horse remained on the take-off side. Huw groaned again. One by one, Huw's horses fell out of contention. Each time one of Huw's horses departed the race, I heard him groan.

I don't know if you remember the 1963 Grand National. It was won by a horse named Ayala, which started at odds of 66/1. There was a very exciting finish to the race, with Ayala getting up to win in the final few strides, but I don't think Huw was watching. None of his horses was involved in the finish.

"Why didn't you back Ayala, Huw?" I asked him. For a moment I thought Huw was going to share some confidence with me, but he seemed to think better of it. "You can't back them all, Gareth," was all he said.

In the aftermath of the race we learned that Ayala's chances had been dismissed even by his trainer. The horse had been entered in the Grand National only to please his owner, who was a famous hairdresser who rejoiced in the nom de plume 'Teasy Weasy' Raymond. Huw said he'd never heard of him.

When we watched the re-run of the race we saw that Ayala had ploughed through a fence on the first circuit, practically uprooting it. It was a miracle that he'd stayed upright. Then, when it came to the same fence on the second circuit, the horse headed straight for the gap he'd made the first time around, not even having to lift his feet up as he went through it. "Is that legal, Huw?" I asked. But Huw seemed lost in thought; he didn't answer me.

Young as I was, I understood that that race was a chastening experience for Huw. It seemed to have knocked his confidence, and over the next two or three years I could feel my relationship with him subtly altering. I still cycled out to Bow Street as often as I could, but Huw no longer appeared quite the font of wisdom that I'd taken him for earlier. Nonetheless, he continued to advise me on the dangers and pitfalls of life. In particular, he would warn me against drinking alcohol. "Gareth," he'd say to me, "I've seen more good men ruined through drink than anything else. You keep away from it, my boy."

I was fifteen when Huw gave me that warning, and apart from one mouthful of champagne at Christmas, which was the foulest thing I'd ever tasted, I'd never touched alcohol. But I knew Huw was fond of me and I appreciated the fact that he wanted to protect me from developing bad habits.

Huw himself preferred tea to alcohol. He would drink several cups in the couple of hours that I spent with him. "You see this stuff… " he'd say, pointing to the whisky bottle from which he poured a measure into each cup, "never touch it my boy. At my age it's necessary in order to keep awake, but it would be the ruination of a young chap like you. Best if you keep away from it altogether."

Huw was finding it more and more difficult to keep awake. Sometimes he fell fast asleep whilst Owen and I were with him in the cottage. If Huw nodded off whilst Owen or I were there, we would put a blanket over his knees and then turn out the light before tiptoeing out of the cottage and cycling home. We never told mam that we sometimes left Huw fast asleep in his cottage. If she'd known, she might not have let us visit him any more.

"Tell them, Meurig," I heard her say to my father one day, "it can't be good for them to see Huw in that state."

But although mam didn't like me and Owen going to see Huw, she never actually stopped us. Perhaps she didn't know we went as often as we did.

It was a few weeks after I overheard that conversation between my parents that I cycled out to see Huw once more. It had been a longer break than usual because by this time I was playing rugby for the school most Saturdays.

Huw seemed more pleased to see me than ever. "Been getting myself in a right mess," he said, pointing to a mound of dirty dishes and some rather grubby-looking blankets scattered about the room. He laughed as he said it, but he didn't seem very happy to me. He looked as if he hadn't shaved for several days, and the cottage was smelly.

After I'd found a seat, Huw looked at me without speaking for a moment. Then he said:

"Tell me Gareth, do you ever get fed up?"

"Sometimes," I said, "when mam's cross."

"Do you ever get sad and lonely?"

"No," I told him, "I don't think so."

"Good!" exclaimed Huw. "Glad to hear it. I've got something to say to you, Gareth – something I'd like you to remember. It's just in case there comes a time when you feel a bit down in the dumps. Do you think you can imagine the sort of feeling I mean?"

I nodded.

"All right. Well, what I want to say to you is this..."

Huw paused and looked at me sternly.

"Never give up!"

He said it so fiercely that I jumped.

"You'll have people depending on you," Huw went on. "No matter how bad you feel, just remember that the bad times won't last. Do you understand, Gareth?"

I nodded again.

"Good. That's enough of my lecturing. Let's have a cup of tea."

When I got home I spoke to my mother about Huw.

"Mam," I said, "I think Huw's fed up."

"Humph! Of course he's fed up," she said, "sitting in that cottage all day long. He's only himself to blame."

I don't know that anyone was to blame, but that Saturday was the last time I saw Huw. My father broke the news to Owen and me when we came home from school the following Monday. Dad was looking at us both as if to gauge our reaction, but neither Owen nor I said very much. I don't think either of us was surprised.

I used to think that mam didn't like Huw, but she seemed almost as upset as my dad. That evening I heard the two of them talking together.

"Meurig," my mother said, "do you suppose Huw told Gareth what he was going to do?"

"I shouldn't think so," my father replied. "Huw would have had more sense than to burden Gareth with his troubles."

There was a long pause and I could hear my mother crying.

"Such a pity with them both so fond of him," she said at last. "If only he'd thought what an example he was setting the boys."

The Golfer and his Caddie

IN THE EARLY spring of 1963, when the Beetles' 'Please Please Me' was riding high in the charts and I was in the fifth form at Ardwyn, a friend of my father's gave Owen and me some cast-off golf clubs. This was not an excessively generous gift; the clubs were old – antique, even – with wooden shafts, while the metal of the club heads was ringed with rust. Still, the clubs were serviceable, more or less, and when that winter's bitter cold had finally relented, Owen and I got into the habit of wandering on to the golf course near our home to hit a few balls. We went at the end of the day, when the light was fading and the course was otherwise deserted, because we knew the golf course was private land on which we were trespassing. On a few occasions we were spotted by members, and yelled at.

After a few weeks of this illicit golfing activity, Owen and I applied to join the club as junior members. It was good to be able to play in daylight, without being shouted at. Some of the adult members took a friendly interest in these young kids who were learning the game, but neither Owen nor I had formal instruction. We both enjoyed bashing the ball and, despite the limitations of our equipment, we were able to hit it quite a long way. That was what we enjoyed the most – there was nothing subtle about the way either of us approached the game.

Owen also developed a related interest, which I didn't share. He loved hunting for golf balls, and would spend hours wandering the further reaches of the golf course, where the grass grew long. The members grew used to seeing Owen wandering along, his eyes glued to the ground, seeking out telltale specks of white. It seemed to me that Owen had an almost mystical talent for finding golf balls. I hardly found any, but Owen supplied us both. He and I would also lose balls, since our ball striking was highly erratic, but Owen found far more than he lost. He had an instinctive sense of the places around the course where golf balls were to be found.

One of Owen's favourite haunts was a disused quarry that lay about a mile from our house, beside the 17th fairway. The 17th fairway was narrow, only about thirty yards across, and the quarry lay beyond the perimeter fence. It was out of bounds for golfers, but the prevailing wind blew in that direction and high handicappers were forever slicing their drive into its cavernous depths. Owen knew this, and he made frequent visits to the quarry, whence he would return with a rich haul of golf balls, many of them in pristine condition. Occasionally, members who had driven into the quarry would scale the perimeter fence and clamber down the steep shale incline in an attempt to retrieve their ball. They had to be quick if they were to get there before Owen. Sometimes golfers would make the descent into the quarry only to find Owen wandering innocently amongst the rocks. "Have you seen my ball?" they would enquire, and Owen would shake his head mournfully, in silent commiseration for their loss.

Owen and I were both awarded a golf handicap, which in theory enabled us to play in competitions. Owen's handicap was 30 and mine was 36, which was the highest permissible. I'm not sure how it was that I came to have a higher handicap than Owen; I thought we were as bad as each other. Maybe the handicap committee spotted some potential in Owen that they reckoned was absent in my case. And it's true that in time, to the surprise of some of those who knew him as a thirteen year old, Owen became quite an accomplished amateur golfer.

I never did. I only remained a member of Aberystwyth Golf Club for twelve months, in which time I never once managed to go round in fewer than a hundred strokes. I was too stubborn to apply myself properly, and because I was self-taught I developed bad habits which proved impossible to eradicate. My only hope of competitive success lay in handicap competitions – 36 strokes is a useful cushion. But I didn't enjoy the so-called 'medal' rounds, where you were required to total up your score over the full eighteen holes. My play was too erratic for me to be able to do myself justice, and anyway the handicap allowance I was afforded struck me as arbitrary and slightly ridiculous. Who could enjoy a 'victory' that was gained only by dint of an enormous bonus?

No, the only competitive success that I gained over my twelve months of membership came in head-to-head matches against opponents who were roughly of my own standard. There was one competition in particular, the Bill Owen Trophy, for golfers with a handicap of 24 or more, that I like to think saw me at my best. In the Bill Owen there was no handicap allowance. I preferred that. Also, the knockout format suited me because if you ran up an enormous score on one hole – say, a 12 – it meant simply that you lost that hole; it didn't ruin your whole round. For golfers of my standard, that was a considerable benefit.

And there were many golfers of my standard at the Aberystwyth club. Bill Owen himself was one such, and it was very good of Bill to purchase a trophy and give his name to a competition for bad golfers; I don't think that's how I would have wanted to be remembered. Not that Bill accepted his status as a terrible golfer. Like the rest of us, Bill was seeking to improve. He frequently sought advice from the club professional, a sardonic character by the name of Ray Jones. Ray had a slow, lazy swing, and he hit every shot as if he were gently caressing the ball. It was far removed from the way Bill – or indeed I – played the game. Ray must have been in his sixties when I first met him, and he spent most of the time in his shop. When he played, which was seldom, he sent the ball unerringly down the middle of the fairway.

I once stood and watched as Ray gave Bill a lesson. Bill was hitting practice balls into the net that was erected beside the first tee. He launched himself at the ball as if seeking to drive it into the next county, whilst Ray looked on impassively, saying nothing. After a while Bill paused in his flailing and looked hopefully at his mentor. "Well?" he enquired. Ray pondered. "Have you thought of hitting it with your back swing?" he asked. "Eh?" said Bill. "You're swinging a bit fast."

The one time I entered the Bill Owen Trophy I was drawn in the first round to play against a local businessman by the name of Mike Forrest. Mike was wealthy, or at least appeared to be. He had a car dealership in the town, but that wasn't all; Mike had a finger in a great many pies.

I was wary of Mike Forrest. He drove a Jaguar with a personalised number plate, and he was a fierce adversary of my mother. When we first came to Aberystwyth, Mike had lived a few doors away from us, and he and my parents had had a quarrel. The argument had been over repairs to our road. According to my mother, Mike had refused to pay his share of the work that needed to be done. As a result of this, our road, which was privately owned, had for some years been in a state of disrepair. When there was a storm, as happened frequently in Aberystwyth, some of the road surface would be washed down the hill towards the town. Whenever this happened, mam would call Mike Forrest all sorts of names. Even after Mike had moved to another part of town, and our road was given a proper tarmacadam dressing, mam would shudder with rage at the mention of his name.

Dad also considered that Mike had behaved badly, but he felt less strongly on the matter, as was his way. He and Mike were civil towards one another, but if mam encountered Mike Forrest on the streets of Aberystwyth, she would cross the road to avoid him. My mother did not readily abandon her grievances, and Mike Forrest was top of her list.

I was too young to have known very much about the quarrel concerning the road, and it didn't affect me, but I was wary of Mike for another reason. This is something that is only ever whispered in golf clubs, but I'd heard other members talk about Mike in a way that implied he couldn't be trusted to keep an accurate count of his shots. I had no direct experience of this – I hadn't played a round with Mike, and we hadn't done more than nod to one another – but I knew it was said, and there was something about Mike that suggested to me it might be true.

Shortly before Mike and I were due to play our match, I was stood on the steps of Ray Jones' shop as he watched Mike engage in a series of vigorous practice swings. Good golfers give the appearance of effortlessly sweeping the ball to a distant horizon. Mike swung as if taking an axe to a recalcitrant tree stump. Ray sighed.

"If I had a swing like that," he muttered, "I wouldn't practise it."

He looked at me reflectively.

"When are you playing your match?"

"Next Tuesday."

"Have you got a caddie?"

I shook my head.

"Why not ask Owen?"

It hadn't occurred to me that I needed a caddie, and that was all Ray Jones said on the matter, but it felt as though he was giving me a piece of friendly advice. I only had five golf clubs, and my bag certainly wasn't heavy, but Ray wouldn't have suggested it unless he thought that having Owen caddie for me would be useful. I spoke to Owen that evening.

"What are you doing next Tuesday?" I asked.

"Going to school, same as you."

"Will you caddie for me later when I play Mike Forrest?"

Owen gave the matter some thought, before nodding gravely.

"An adventure," he murmured.

When Tuesday came I was unexpectedly nervous. I knew my mother was desperate for me to beat Mike Forrest, and I was worried about letting her down. Owen, however, seemed confident. When our dad asked him how he rated my chances, he replied: "Gareth is bad, but Mike Forrest is worse." With Owen's endorsement ringing in my ears, he and I set off for the golf course. I carried my own bag; after all, Owen wasn't my servant.

When we arrived, Mike Forrest was smacking balls into the practice net that stood beside the first tee. He glanced at Owen but made no comment regarding his presence. He looked at his watch. It seemed he was anxious to start. "Right," he said, "it's five o'clock. Time to get going. Let's toss for it." Mike spun a coin in the air. I called correctly, so I had the 'honour' off the first tee. I'd hoped to have a few practice swings, but it was plain from Mike's demeanour that he considered the time for practising had passed. The three of us clambered up the short gravel path to the competition tee, and I surveyed the scene. The first hole at Aberystwyth is long – at least 420 yards – and there is out of bounds to the right. To the left is the clubhouse. I didn't dare look, but I felt certain that curious eyes were watching us.

"What ball are you using?" I asked Mike Forrest.

"Dunlop 65, number 3. You?"

"Gambit, number 4."

I had better balls in my bag than that scuffed old Gambit, but I didn't trust myself. There was no point taking an expensive new ball and depositing it in the woods, and until I brought my nerves under control goodness knows where my ball would end up.

"Better take an iron," I said to Owen, "for safety."

Owen handed over my 3 iron. I could tell by his impassive demeanour that he was trying to transmit a sense of calm. I certainly needed it; my hands were sweaty on the leather grip of my golf club.

I took a deep breath as I contemplated the shimmering white object at my feet. I stood there for what seemed like minutes, but I guess it was only a second or two; then I launched. I looked up to follow the flight of the ball, but I was too early – the effect of that premature lifting of my head was to raise the trajectory of the golf club, which in consequence did no more than graze the roof of the ball, generating just sufficient momentum to cause it to trickle down the gravel path that we'd ascended a few moments earlier. Owen and I peered over the lip of the tee. My ball was in clear view, nestling at the foot of the path, having travelled less than twenty yards. "Safe enough," said Owen.

Then it was Mike Forrest's turn. Somewhat to my surprise he seemed as nervous as me. He selected his driver and engaged in several fierce waggles of the club head. Those preliminaries concluded, his technique thereafter comprised an exaggerated pause at the top of the back swing, followed by a steep downward lunge. Subjected to this unkind treatment, Mike's ball performed a vicious left to right parabola before disappearing into the woods that bounded the first fairway. "Buggeration!" That was Mike's favourite expletive, commonly heard around the golf course.

Mike fished in his bag for another ball and set himself again.

His swing on this second occasion seemed to me identical to his first, but this time the trajectory was from right to left. Mike's ball screamed through the practice putting green beside the clubhouse, skipped across the 15th green and disappeared in the direction of the 16th tee. Muttering to himself, Mike slammed his driver into his bag and headed off to the 16th. As he passed the clubhouse I heard a cheer and a flutter of ironic applause. Our round had begun.

Mike Forrest's progress up the first was largely hidden from view because his route took him up the 15th fairway. This in turn meant that he faced a demanding cross-country passage though thick rough in order to arrive in the vicinity of the first green. Owen and I decided we had no option but to continue on our way up the first fairway. My nerves having settled somewhat, I made relatively serene progress up the first, depositing my ball on the green with my fifth stroke. It was some time before Mike appeared, his arrival heralded by the sound of his ball thudding into a greenside bunker. "How many shots is that?" I asked him. "Five," pronounced Mike. Owen looked at me quizzically, but I couldn't challenge Mike's arithmetic when he'd spent almost the entire hole out of sight. "I'm on for five," I told him.

Not that it mattered. Mike's effort in the bunker was probably the best shot he'd played for some time. It might have had a satisfactory outcome had his club head entered the sand a few inches behind the ball, as he'd intended, but Mike connected clean as a whistle, sending his ball steepling over the fence that bounded the second fairway. He must have hit it the best part of 200 yards, which is an impressive hit out of sand, although not ideal when you're in a greenside bunker. "Buggeration!" exclaimed Mike, followed shortly by, "I concede."

Mike and I shared the next two holes. I went out of bounds on the second, but I recovered my advantage on the third when Mike hit his ball under a gorse bush and attempted to play the ball where it lay, rather than taking a penalty drop. Mike's first two attempts to extricate his ball were unsuccessful, and by the time he'd finished there wasn't much left of that gorse bush.

The fourth hole at Aberystwyth is challenging, with a large area of deep rough to be traversed from the tee. For once I hit a decent drive, and I breathed a sigh of relief as my ball crept onto the fairway, just visible beyond the brow of the hill. Then it was Mike's turn. The waggling seemed to go on even longer than usual, following which he launched himself at the ball with characteristic fury. Had it been a clean strike, Mike's ball would doubtless have gone a long way, but he must have had his eyes shut at the moment of impact because his ball glanced off the heel of his club and flew in the direction of a clump of reeds, about a hundred yards to our left. The chances of any of us finding Mike's ball in that muck seemed to me remote, but I knew I should offer to help. "Would you like us to help you look?" I enquired. "No, you go on," Mike replied, "I'll just give it a few minutes."

Owen and I trudged over the brow of the hill. Just as we reached my ball, there came a cry from Mike: "Found it!" I glanced at Owen. "Impressive," he murmured. A few seconds later Mike Forrest's ball came whistling over our heads. "Must have found a nice lie," said Owen.

I messed up the remainder of the fourth. I was on the green in three shots, but the fourth green slopes steeply from back to front and I took four putts to get down. Mike and I were level again. I was fuming, but Owen gave no sign of having noticed anything untoward. He was very polite to Mike.

The fifth hole began well, but in the end proved to be another disaster for me. Mike hooked his drive so far into the rough separating the fifth and sixth fairways that I assumed his ball was gone for good, but after a few minutes the cry of "Found it!" echoed once more across the course. I was so taken aback that

I over-hit my approach to the fifth green, sending my ball clean over the hedge behind the green and into a private garden. That, of course, incurred a two-shot penalty, and although Mike took 7, he still won the hole. I needed to get a grip of myself. I was too preoccupied with what Mike was up to; it was beginning to affect my game.

Ahead for the first time in the match, Mike displayed an unaccustomed jauntiness as he made his way along the path to the sixth tee. "Great life if you don't weaken," he announced to no-one in particular. The sixth was another long hole, more or less parallel to the fifth but running in the opposite direction. Mike's drive was another of his specials, a duck hook that plunged into the expanse of rough separating the two fairways. "I'll help you find it," said Owen. "No, don't worry," Mike said to him, "look after your man." But Owen was off. He didn't even wait for me to take my drive. Dumping my golf bag at my feet, he marched after Mike's ball.

Owen spent several minutes helping Mike search for his ball whilst I, feeling rather disgruntled at having been abandoned by Owen in this unceremonious fashion, plotted a zigzag course up the sixth fairway. It was only after Owen had returned to my side that we heard Mike's familiar cry of "Found it!" "A miracle," breathed Owen.

The sixth hole was halved, so Mike was still one up as we confronted the formidable challenge of the seventh. The seventh hole at Aberystwyth is superficially inviting, being a downhill par 3, but it nonetheless strikes fear into the hearts of high handicap golfers because their drive has to cross 180 yards of what is, to all intents and purposes, a swamp. Mike having retained the honour, he was first to drive. Owen and I stood and watched as Mike's waggling of the club head seemed to go on for ever. It didn't help him much: when he finally launched himself at the ball, he sent his drive spiralling away to an area some sixty yards left of the green where the reeds grew tall. In terms of accuracy, it was one of his better efforts, but he could hardly have found a worse spot. I too missed the fairway, but I sliced my drive away to the right, where the ground was comparatively dry.

As he had done on the sixth, Owen abandoned me in favour of helping Mike hunt for his ball. It was several minutes before he wandered across to where I was standing. "Pretty swampy in there," he observed cheerfully. At that moment there came the familiar cry from Mike: "Found it!" "Another miracle," whispered Owen. But Mike's miracle was to no avail. His second shot failed to dislodge his ball from the reeds. "Buggeration!" he exclaimed again. His next attempt sent his ball careering across the green into another patch of deep rough. "Hole conceded," announced Mike.

The pattern of the round had been set. Mike continued to visit the further reaches of the golf course, with Owen in dogged attendance. Somewhat to my surprise Owen never once found Mike's ball, but apart from the ones he hit out of bounds Mike himself enjoyed a 100 per cent success rate.

It was on the 13th hole that I first detected a change in Mike's mood. He was still in the lead, but when his drive at the 13th plummeted into the left-hand rough, Mike, accompanied by the faithful Owen, spent an unaccustomed length of time searching for his ball. It was some considerable time after Owen had returned to my side that Mike called across: "I think I'll concede this one." Delighted at this unexpected bonus, I picked up my ball and followed Owen as he trudged in the direction of the 14th tee. As I caught up with Owen he whispered something that I didn't quite catch. "What did you say?" I asked him. Owen looked at me impatiently. His voice was barely audible. "He's running out of balls," he whispered.

The end of the match came unexpectedly, at least as far as I was concerned. We'd halved the 14th, which is the easiest hole on the golf course, and were now confronted by the 15th, which in most people's eyes is the hardest. Over 500 yards in length, with a narrow fairway bounded on both sides by deep rough, the 15th descends steeply to a plateau green surrounded by deep sand bunkers. Afflicted once more by nerves, I scuffed my drive, which just crept onto the fairway. As had been the pattern for the previous few holes, Mike sent his ball careering into the left-hand rough. Resignedly accepting the attentions of the faithful Owen, he set off in pursuit.

Once again Owen failed to find Mike's ball, and as had been the case on the 13th it seemed that Mike too was out of luck. After five minutes or so Owen abandoned the search, but Mike spent several more minutes wandering back and forth. Eventually he called across: "This old shoulder of mine is playing up. I'm going to have to concede the match."

"No more balls," whispered Owen. I was dumbfounded. A wave of relief swept over me. I'd been anticipating a tough duel over the closing holes. Mike made his way over to where Owen and I were standing. Gingerly he held out his hand. "Hard luck," I said. Mike also shook hands with Owen. "Hard luck," said Owen, "I hope your shoulder is better soon."

When we got home and I told our parents that Mike Forrest had conceded the match on the 15th, mam gave me a hug that seemed to go on forever. "My brilliant boy!" she said. Dad was more interested in the sporting aspects of the win. "How did Gareth play?" he asked Owen. "He was terrible," Owen replied, "but Mike Forrest was worse."

Later that evening, as Owen and I were getting ready for bed, I saw him rummaging through the pockets of his waterproof jacket. He passed the jacket to me. "What's this for?" I asked him. "Look in the pockets," Owen replied. I felt in the pockets of Owen's jacket and emptied the contents onto my bed. There were six golf balls, all Dunlop 65s. They seemed to be practically brand-new. “Where did you get these?” I asked him. “I found them, out on the course. You can have three of them if you like.”

That was the first and last time Owen caddied for me. I might have asked him to perform the same service in the next round, but I didn’t want to impose upon him. Anyway, I was drawn to play against Ron Thompson, one of the older members, a gentleman who was always friendly towards me, and I thought I could manage well enough on my own.

As it happens I lost that second-round match, but it had nothing to do with having to carry my own clubs. I just didn’t play very well, and Ron was a much better golfer than Mike Forrest. When it came to the end of the year, I opted not to renew my membership of Aberystwyth Golf Club. Golf wasn’t my game, and I didn’t enjoy it nearly as much without Owen on my bag. That win over Mike Forrest proved to be the summit of my golfing career.

Saturday Night

SEX AND ROMANCE didn't come easily to me when I was eighteen. Perhaps being brought up in Aberystwyth had something to do with it. As my friend Emyr said to me once: "Gareth, the birds in this place couldn't make a monk feel randy." I agreed with him at the time, but it was sour grapes, as I'm sure you know. Neither of us had a girlfriend. Emyr talked a lot about girls, but I don't think his experience was any greater than mine.

Emyr and I would usually meet on a Saturday night in The Crown, which at that time was one of the most popular pubs in Aberystwyth. "Those Ceredigion virgins had better look out tonight," Emyr would say. Ceredigion was the largest of the university halls of residence for female students. Neither Emyr nor I thought to mention our own sexual inexperience, which in my case was total.

Emyr would say to me: "I'm not looking for the girl I'll marry, tonight." That was Emyr's catchphrase. We both knew the kind of girl he *was* looking for. Not that he had any hope of finding her. I suppose you might say that we exhibited a bit of a double standard in our attitude to girls of our acquaintance, although I doubt we were any worse than most other boys of our age.

It was at this delicate stage of my sexual development that I encountered Sonia Watkins. Sonia went to Ardwyn, the same as me, but a year behind. She wore glasses the same as I did and she was taller than I liked – about two inches taller than me, in fact. But then most girls were taller than me. Sonia's impact on me was like the promise of rain to a man dying of thirst in the Sahara. When she looked at you it was with a look that promised… well, I wasn't sure what Sonia promised, but she had me in the palm of her hand.

It happened one Saturday night. Emyr and I were sitting in The Crown, planning our evening's activities. I saw him pat his jacket pocket. He had a contraceptive in there. It was more of a good luck charm than anything else – Emyr had never had cause to use it. His brother had given it to him and it must have been a bit ancient by this time, but Emyr took it with him on Saturday nights in case his prayers were answered.

I was wondering whether I had too much aftershave on. I didn't really need to shave, but I used to have a scrape occasionally in the hope of encouraging growth, and I'd just started to use aftershave. I hoped it would turn every girl within range into a helpless victim of overwhelming desire. Emyr said he was embarrassed in case people thought it was him who smelt like that. But Sonia must have liked it.

She walked into The Crown that evening with another girl from school. We were sitting near the bar and Emyr asked the girls if he could buy them a drink. I remember that Sonia had a lager and lime. That was the drink most girls used to ask for at that time.

Sonia and her friend came to sit with us and Sonia sat next to me. We'd been sat there for a few minutes and I was worried I hadn't said anything. Then Sonia turned to me:

"Well, well, so *you're* Gareth Jenkins," she said.

"Yes," I said.

Not exactly wonderful as conversation goes.

"I've heard a lot about you," Sonia said.

"Have you? What have you heard then?"

"Never you mind. But Emyr's told me a few things."

"Hey, Emyr!" I said. "What have you told Sonia about me?" I was glad of the chance to speak to Emyr. Sonia made me feel a bit uncomfortable, sitting so close and talking straight at me like that.

"I told her you were the best shove ha-penny player in school," said Emyr.

As a matter of fact that's true about me being a good shove ha-penny player. I was pleased that Emyr had told Sonia that. Suddenly I felt something soft and warm pressing against my right arm. I looked down. It was Sonia's left breast.

"Um… do you know how to play shove ha-penny?" I asked.

I must have been a bit red as I said it, but Sonia didn't seem to notice.

"No," she said. "Tell me what you do."

So I told Sonia a bit about shove ha-penny. I was glad to have something to talk about. I know now that it isn't a good idea to talk for too long about something like shove ha-penny when you first meet a girl, but I was nervous so I seized on the first topic that presented itself. My hand shook when I picked up my drink.

When I couldn't think of anything more to say about shove ha-penny, I looked round at Emyr. He was still talking to the other girl.

"Do you smoke?" Sonia asked me.

"Yes," I said. I find I generally lie when I'm asked something quick.

"Have you got a fag?" she asked.

"No – but I'll get some if you like."

"OK. There's a machine outside. I'll come with you."

As Sonia and I got up to go outside, Emyr looked at me.

"Where are you going, boy?" he said.

"For a walk," Sonia told him.

"Only to get some fags," I said. "Back in a minute."

"Oh indeed!" said Emyr. "Well, enjoy your smoke, Gareth boy. Watch he only takes little puffs," he added to Sonia.

I think Emyr was jealous. Sonia ignored him. As we walked out of the pub Emyr was making a rude sign at me. I don't think Sonia noticed. When we got outside she surprised me by saying: "Let's walk for a bit."

"Don't you want to smoke?" I asked.

"No," she said. "Come on."

So we went for a walk. We walked down to the harbour, which in Aberystwyth is a place that couples often go to in their cars. Perhaps all harbours are like that. I knew I could hold Sonia's hand if I wanted to, but for some reason I didn't dare. It's funny how sometimes you're afraid to do things even when you know the other person wants you to.

When we got to the harbour we stood by the railings and looked at the sea. Then Sonia turned to me.

"You're shy, aren't you?" she murmured.

"Not really," I said.

The next thing I knew, Sonia moved closer towards me. I made a sudden lurch and our spectacles crashed together. I may have talked a lot to Emyr about girls, but I'd hardly kissed one before – not properly.

"Don't worry," Sonia said, and she took her glasses off. It was all right after that. We must have stayed by the harbour for about an hour. It was dark and the night was cold and quite windy, so there weren't many people about. It was freezing as a matter of fact, but I enjoyed kissing Sonia and I had a kind of proud and pleased feeling that I *was* kissing her, if you know what I mean.

After a while I could feel Sonia shivering and I asked if she'd like me to take her home. She seemed quite glad that I'd suggested it. We held hands as we walked. When we reached her house I asked if I could see her again next week.

"Do you really want to?" she asked.

"You bet," I said.

"All right then. Saturdays are best."

I felt so excited and pleased that I ran all the way home. I wondered what Emyr would have to say about it.

Emyr had quite a lot to say as it turned out. I saw him in school on Monday.

"Gareth boy," he said to me, "you've got it made. Did you see that look in her eyes? She's crazy about you."

I don't suppose Emyr had ever looked in Sonia's eyes, but all the same I was pleased when he said that.

"Don't talk soft," I said. "How can you tell?"

"The old intuition, boy… vibrations."

Well, I knew how much notice to take of Emyr's vibrations.

"You'd better be prepared next time," he said to me.

"What do you mean – 'prepared'?" I asked him.

"Like the scouts, boy – or we'll have another little Gareth Jenkins on our hands nine months from now."

"Don't be daft," I said.

It was a thought, all the same. We started to walk in the direction of our homes.

"You could lend me yours," I said to him.

Emyr's reaction was more or less what I expected. He clutched his forehead and pretended to stagger across the road.

"Don't tell me, Gareth boy," he said, "I suppose you'll give it back to me when you've finished with it."

Of course I'd meant no such thing.

"All right then," I said, "I'll buy it off you."

"No thanks," said Emyr, "it's got sentimental value. Anyway, I might need it myself."

"I don't believe you've still got it," I said.

"Don't you? What's this do you think?"

He fished out a crumpled object from his pocket. He must have carried it with him everywhere. It looked a bit worn but I could tell it was the real thing.

"Let's have a look," I said.

Rather suspiciously Emyr handed over the contraceptive. I examined it carefully.

"Have you read what it says here?" I asked him.

"What do you mean? Here – give it back!"

"Listen to this," I said, holding it away from him. "Not to be used after 1962. Emyr, your contraceptive is out of date. It must be at least ten years old. It'll fall apart if you try to use it."

"Don't talk rot. It's like the dates they put on food. It's perfectly OK to eat them afterwards."

"That may be all right for dried milk," I told him, "but not for contraceptives. Ceri must have got this in an antique shop. It should be in an exhibition."

Emyr snatched it back.

"That's OK," he said, "I wouldn't have given it to you anyway."

We walked on a little further.

"I'll tell you what, boy. They sell them in machines, you know."

He was right of course. Some gents' toilets had contraceptive machines.

"All you've got to do when you're in the pub with Sonia next Saturday is to pop into the gents and get some out of the machine."

"What pubs do they have them in?" I asked Emyr. "I haven't noticed them in The Crown."

"I think they've got one in The Coach and Horses," he said. "And if they haven't got one in there, I'm pretty sure they've got a machine in The Talbot. I think that's where Ceri got his."

I called for Sonia at seven o'clock the following Saturday. I'd spotted her a few times in the week, talking to other girls, but I hadn't had the nerve to approach her. I didn't know if she was officially my girlfriend, and I wasn't sure how I was supposed to behave if she was. It was as if the Sonia of last Saturday night had no connection with the young woman laughing and joking with her classmates. All my confidence had evaporated.

It revived a bit when Sonia answered her front door – I was afraid that I'd be confronted by Mr Watkins, who would issue me with a stern warning to stop pestering his daughter.

We went to The Crown first off. It was sort of automatic; I always went there on Saturday nights. When Sonia took her coat off in The Crown I saw she had a low-cut dress on underneath. I found it difficult to talk to her sensibly. I'd forgotten all about that ridiculous conversation with Emyr, but now I found myself wondering – what if he'd been right? Maybe, for once in his life, he hadn't been talking nonsense.

It was only a few minutes after I'd bought Sonia a drink that Emyr showed up, like a bad penny. He came over to speak to us.

"Come to pick up some tips," he said.

After a few minutes of listening to Emyr rabbiting on I went to the gents. I didn't need the toilet but I checked to see if there was a contraceptive machine lurking somewhere. There wasn't.

When I got back I asked Sonia if she'd like to go to another pub. "Try The Coach and Horses," said Emyr. "Worth it just for the gents."

Sonia looked a bit surprised. "I'd rather stay here for a bit, if you don't mind," she said.

I didn't know what to do. Naturally, I couldn't force her to go to another pub if she didn't want to. I bought Sonia another drink and I bought Emyr one as well, though I wished he'd go away. Then I had an idea. The Coach and Horses was only a hundred yards away. I could say that I was going to the gents and then nip outside and run to get the contraceptive.

I stood up as if to go to the toilet once more.

"Won't be a minute," I said.

"But you've only just been," Sonia complained.

"Bladder like a sieve," said Emyr as I headed for the door. "Due for the operation any day."

I walked straight through the toilets in The Crown and out onto the street. Then I ran as hard as I could to The Coach and Horses. There was hardly anyone in the pub. I tried not to look at the barman as I went straight past him into the gents. There was no contraceptive machine that I could see – only one old chap having a pee.

I tried to go too, just to make it look right, but it was difficult I can tell you. I had to go through the bar again on my way out, which was embarrassing because the barman spoke to me this time.

"This isn't a public convenience, you know," he said.

"Sorry," I said, "I thought it was from the outside."

People are always complaining about silly things like that. I'd hardly used his stupid toilet, anyway.

When I got out into the street I didn't know what to do. It was time I got back to Sonia, but I thought this might be my last chance. I didn't hesitate for long. The Talbot was in the next street. I ran there as fast as I could. The lounge bar was empty except for one couple sitting in the corner. The barman was Jack Phillips, a friend of my father's. I walked through the bar as fast as I could, but Jack spotted me.

"Don't see you here very often, Gareth," he said. "What'll it be?"

There was no escape.

"Half a bitter please, Jack," I said.

"Go on, have a pint. You're old enough."

So Jack poured me a pint. I could see he wanted to talk, but I was getting a bit frantic. I took a couple of sips and headed for the gents.

The first thing I noticed was the contraceptive machine. There was no-one else there. I examined my change. I only had one half crown piece. I put it into the machine. As I did so I heard someone coming along the passage to the toilet. I shot across to the urinal. I stared at the wall as the door opened behind me. It was the bloke who'd been sitting in the lounge bar with his girlfriend. He went over to the contraceptive machine. I heard him pull the lever and then the contraceptive must have dropped down because he laughed. I glanced round and saw him pocket it before he turned and walked out again. I thought of shouting at him – "That's mine!" – but it was too late. Anyway, I wouldn't have had the nerve. I was in a right state to tell you the truth. I had no more half crowns and Sonia must be wondering where I was.

I went straight through the bar without finishing my drink.

"Got to rush," I said to Jack as I passed him, "late for an appointment."

Jack would probably tell my father, but I hadn't time to worry about that. Anyway, I was telling the truth for once.

As I ran back to The Crown I thought how difficult it was to do something as simple as buy a contraceptive. I was also trying to work out how I'd explain to Sonia about my being in the gents for so long.

I needn't have bothered. Just before I got to The Crown I saw Sonia. She was walking away from me on the opposite side of the road, and she was with someone else. Then the two of them crossed the road and I could see they were holding hands. I could see who the other person was, as well. It was Emyr.

I stood and watched until they turned a corner and were out of sight. I didn't move or call out. I suppose I could have gone up to them and said what I thought, but I didn't bother. I could have made a few sarcastic remarks about Emyr's ancient contraceptive, but I didn't do that either.

In the end I went back to The Crown. It was more crowded than when I'd left, but I noticed Sonia's friend from last weekend stood by the bar. I remembered that her name was Christine.

"You look flushed," she said to me.

"Comes of visiting too many toilets," I told her.

There were a lot of people in The Crown, and Christine and I found ourselves pressed together.

"Would you like a drink?" I asked her.

"Yes, please!"

She made it sound as if she were really glad to be asked.

"I'll try to find us a seat," she said – and she smiled. I hadn't noticed it before, but she had a very nice smile.

The Voice of Experience

THE LOCAL NEWSPAPER in that part of Cardiganshire where I grew up was called *The Welsh Gazette*. A distinctive feature of the paper at that time was that the editor allocated two columns each week to a celebrated local short story writer. His pen name was 'Dafydd' and every week he would produce a story of about 1,000 words. Some of what Dafydd wrote was clearly fiction, or so it seemed to me – it was certainly implausible – and some was a commentary on local events.

Dafydd's column did not hold great appeal for me; his stories were too heavy-handed for my taste, and they nearly always had a moral tacked on at the end. You probably know the kind I mean. Dafydd's specialty was a nostalgic account of Cardiganshire life from another era, with many of those featured having suffered a tragic end, usually in one of the great wars. Or perhaps some local worthy was deprived of the recognition that was rightfully his, and Dafydd was correcting the deficiency. He clouted you over the head with the moral of his story, although of course it was meant to be so subtle that you thought it developed naturally out of the tale he was telling.

Dafydd died the summer I left school and so his column was discontinued. I went to university and only saw *The Welsh Gazette* when I returned home in the holidays. By then I'd started to write a few stories of my own. When I'd written seven or eight I sent them to the proprietor of *The Welsh Gazette*, whose name was Goronwy Ellis-Jones. Mr Ellis-Jones invited me to come to see him when I was next home on holiday. By then I'd written another five pieces, mainly about my student experiences. The stories were meant to be funny, and there was no moral attached to any of them.

Goronwy Ellis-Jones liked my stories. He said he'd need to consult his editor but he would like to publish them. He said it was his policy to try to encourage local talent. I wasn't confident I could be as prolific as Dafydd, so I agreed to write just one column a month. I was to be paid £10 for each one. There was no email or internet in those days, so I used to post the stories home to my mother for her to pass on to the editor, whose name was Joseph Jones. She in turn would send me those copies of *The Welsh Gazette* that contained one of my stories. They were printed on the centre page, where Dafydd's used to be.

After a while I grew tired of writing about my life at university. I began instead to write about some of the ideas I had in my head at that time. My stories became rather esoteric and whimsical. I can see now that I was showing off. My opening paragraphs, in particular, were rambling and self-indulgent. It was sometimes over 200 words before you could tell for certain what I was going to write about – and that, as you probably know, is very bad for a short story, especially one that is going to appear in a newspaper.

When I went home on holiday in the Christmas of my second year at university, Joseph Jones asked me to come to see him. Joseph was a small man with a slight stoop and he had pale blue eyes behind some National Health spectacles of the kind you don't see any more. He told me he thought I was a very promising writer; he said that he hesitated to criticise, but didn't I think that some of my stories were rather rambling? Perhaps, with just 800 words at my disposal, I might consider sharpening up my writing style? Joseph also mentioned – and I think he regarded this as his most serious criticism – that there didn't seem to be a great deal of point to some of my stories. They were quite entertaining, he said, but there was no message for the reader.

I didn't say much to Joseph Jones. I didn't say that I disagreed with his criticism, but then I didn't say that I agreed with it, either. That night I dashed off 800 words about the way people in positions of authority always wanted you to do things their way, and to repeat the mistakes they had made. I found it a very easy piece to write – I write fluently when I have a grievance. I made a few jokes, as I always did, but I can see now that it was a rather juvenile reaction to Joseph's criticism, which had been kindly meant. I called it 'Taking a Liberty' and I sent it to Joseph the next day.

The following evening Joseph Jones telephoned me at home. He said he was sorry that I had responded in that way to my conversation with him. My column wasn't acceptable. He asked me to submit another one, but I refused. I was surprised at myself: although I can be firm in print, I'm usually weak in conversation. But I thought my stance was justified; I wasn't prepared to be told what to write, and my horizons extended far beyond *The Welsh Gazette* – or so I thought at the time. I was a cocky little so-and-so in those days.

A few days after that telephone conversation I received a letter from Goronwy Ellis-Jones. He thanked me for my contribution to *The Welsh Gazette*. He told me that he felt bound to support the editorial policy of Joseph Jones. He liked my stories, but he thought they were no longer appropriate for a local newspaper focussed upon local events. He suggested that perhaps now was the time for me to look further afield. He enclosed a cheque for £25.

It was my first sacking, and the one I most deserved. But at the time I had no regrets. I was glad that I wasn't going to write for *The Welsh Gazette* any more.

I didn't expect to hear further from Goronwy Ellis-Jones, but when I came home in the summer he telephoned me. He said that he'd shown some of my stories to a friend of his. The friend's name was Andrew McKean and he was the editor of *The Western Daily Press*, which in those days was a large circulation provincial newspaper centred on Bristol and the West Country. Mr McKean had told Goronwy Ellis-Jones that he might be able to offer me something. Goronwy Ellis-Jones wished me luck.

So I made a fresh start. I travelled to Bristol to meet Andrew McKean, a giant of a man with a straggly ginger beard and a stomach that overwhelmed his waistband. He had a somewhat distracted air and I was never entirely convinced that Goronwy Ellis-Jones hadn't foisted me upon him, perhaps in return for some favour done in the past. But Mr McKean proved to be a friendly giant and he was true to his word. He and I agreed that I would write a weekly column for *The Western Daily Press*, portraying aspects of student life. Each week I was to deliver 600 words, drawing on a cast of characters who were familiar to me. My column was to be headed 'Student Blues' and would appear under the pseudonym 'Grant Aided'. I look back on it fondly. I wrote for the *Press* for six months until I finished at university – and then I went to live in Bristol and worked full-time on the paper, reporting local news as well as writing the occasional column under my 'Grant Aided' byline.

This should have been just what I was looking for, but I didn't enjoy Bristol as much as I'd expected. I was lonely, and I struggled to write. The reporting side was OK, although far removed from the glamorous image that is sometimes projected of newspaper life, but I had to abandon my column. I was no longer a student, and I'd run out of material. It may just have been a crisis of confidence, but there was nothing I wanted to say – nothing that I felt would be of interest to the *Press* or its readers.

It was about eighteen months after I'd moved to Bristol that I gave up my job at *The Western Daily Press* and returned home. I went to see Goronwy Ellis-Jones and I told him what had happened. I wasn't confident of my reception, but Goronwy Ellis-Jones was a generous man. He offered me a place on *The Welsh Gazette* as a reporter. It wasn't at all the position I'd envisaged for myself when I began posting in my stories, but I was glad to take it.

I found from the beginning that I got on well with Joseph Jones. I discovered that Joseph had qualities that I hadn't appreciated when I was at university. He was far from being an exciting newspaper man, but he was principled, and when he needed to be, he was brave. On two occasions Joseph took on powerful local interests, and was heavily criticised. In both those instances Goronwy Ellis-Jones was asked to intercede, to persuade Joseph to modify his stance, but Joseph stuck to his guns and Goronwy Ellis-Jones refused to sack him.

It was through working with Joseph that I came to understand that reporting on a local newspaper could be an honourable occupation. I no longer worried about my stories; they had their limitations, as I well knew. Instead I did my best to follow Joseph's example and turn myself into a decent local reporter. You could say that has been my goal ever since.

Joseph Jones died last year. He had long since retired, and I hadn't seen him for a while. But I went to his funeral, and I spoke. I said that Joseph had taught me a lot.

As it happens, I'm an editor myself these days. The job doesn't leave much time for writing stories. Or at least, that's what I tell myself. But I know it's not quite right. After all, most of us can find the time to do what we really want to do. Perhaps what I should say is that, as I get older, I find stories more and more difficult to write. It isn't only the opening paragraph that I struggle with nowadays. The greater difficulty lies with my conclusions. Try as I might, I find it hard not to let a moral creep in at the end.